In the Garden

In the Garden

ANTHONY WEBB

IN THE GARDEN

iUniverse books may be ordered through booksellers or by contacting:

iUniverse
1663 Liberty Drive
Bloomington, IN 47403
www.iuniverse.com
1-800-Authors (1-800-288-4677)

ISBN: 978-1-4917-8712-0 (sc)
ISBN: 978-1-4917-8711-3 (hc)
ISBN: 978-1-4917-8710-6 (e)

Library of Congress Control Number: 2016900641

Print information available on the last page.

iUniverse rev. date: 03/10/2016

To Brittany

May your walk IN
your Garden be blessen
and wonderful.

Mr Tony

Chapter 1

Early Morning

Arising from another restless night of unresolved dreams, Mrs. Turner sits on the side of her bed listening to the clock tick down the last minutes of the night. Like a well-tuned timepiece, the birds in the tree outside her bedroom window announce the beginning of a new day by singing their sunrise melody. The morning is about to dawn, whether she is ready for it or not. Lately, sleep has been elusive for Mrs. Turner, causing the nights to become periods in which her thoughts mindlessly wander over past deeds and memories.

Why are these damn birds in that damn mulberry tree so happy this early in the morning? What the heck are they doing? Trying to wake the dead? Shoot, this year, I'm really going to finally have that tree cut down, and then where will they perch their singing butts?

Slowly, a smile comes to her face. *Sometimes them birds aren't so bad. They sound human, like a great choir of souls singing me a song.*

She softly begins to sing. "Soon I will be done with the trouble of this world, the trouble of this world. Soon I will be done with the trouble of this world, going home to live with God. I want to meet my mother. I want to meet my mother ..." and she stops, unable to continue as memories of her mother flood her consciousness. After a moment of reflection, Mrs. Turner wipes her eyes, looks down at her knees, and begins to talk to them. *I hope you old aching knees are still able to carry me, because I have business to do.*

1

Thus begins Mrs. Turner's morning routine: cursing out the birds, limping to the bathroom, and returning back to her room to watch the early edition of the news or some religious program. Today, Mrs. Turner opts for *Rev. Brown's Gospel Hour of Power,* which is really only a half hour program of singing, preaching, and what she calls down-home begging. Rev. Brown's message today is titled "What's Love Got To Do With It?" from the book of 1 John: the love book. Rev. Brown is a master of using powerful intonations to move the congregation to worship. As the camera pans the church, his followers come alive. Shouts of praise fill the sanctuary as Rev. Brown walks back and forth in the pulpit, encouraging his flock to follow Jesus.

Rev. Brown's words find a foothold in Mrs. Turner's soul, stirring a feeling that she thought had been lost years ago. She lets out shouts of "Thank you, Jesus!"

The choir begins to sing, "Jesus is the best thing that ever happened to me," and tears roll down her cheeks.

She starts to sway to the music while singing along with the choir, "Jesus is the best thing that ever happened. Jesus is the best thing that ever happened. Jesus is the best thing that ever happened to me ..."

Today's message has uplifted her spirits, yet it has also exposed feelings that she thought had been buried with her husband two years ago. Although Mrs. Turner was always a believer in God, her spiritual life had suffered greatly with the loss of her husband. His passing revealed she had personal deficiencies that she was not previously aware of. It troubled her that God would allow his death to occur without better preparing her for the pain that was to follow. Mrs. Turner's disappointment in God's actions led her to become spiritually numb, and her husband's death caused her spirit to be absent. Thus, emptiness now filled her. This morning, for the first time in two years, however, she felt a oneness with God. She allowed the old spirit to be renewed, finally feeling whole again. A smile awoke among her tears.

Slowly, she turns her focus back to the television. Rev. Brown had just announced his upcoming revival in Pittsburgh. He closes the program by saying, "You that the Son has set free are free indeed."

"That man sure can preach," Mrs. Turner says aloud.

After the program is over, Mrs. Turner spends some time getting what she calls "reacquainted with her God." She opens her Bible, which lays on the nightstand next to her bed. Old, with tattered edges, it was one of her most prized possessions. Not merely because it contained God's Word. No, it was because it was her father's Bible. Every Sunday morning until his death, her father read to her from this book while sitting under a mulberry tree in their backyard. Her father was able to make the words on those pages come alive, allowing her to visualize the biblical stories. Her favorite story had always been about the three Hebrew boys. Their ability to stand up for what they believed in, despite being at death's doorway, had left an impression on her. Mrs. Turner can remember asking her father why those boys didn't come out of the fiery furnace. The sight of old Ike being roasted at the Fourth of July picnic like an ornery pig was still fresh in her mind. She could not understand why them boys wanted to become BBQ.

Her father rubbed her head and said, "Good question. Sometimes our convictions—those things you believe—are all you have, and when you lose those, you might as well be dead. Or in old Ike's case, become BBQ."

It took Mrs. Turner a while to understand what the heck her father was talking about, but it was a lesson she never forgot. Her thoughts returned to the present and to her sons Jamie, Daniel, Willie, and Rob Jr. Those boys were the loves of her life. She can remember when those four nappy heads were young and into everything. Yes, having her sons set her free. Mrs. Turner never worked outside of the home. While many of her friends viewed the life of a housewife as boring and confining, she loved it. It allowed her to create a world in which the family could thrive and she could govern.

Although the boys were her pride and joy, their maleness did present a problem for her. If they had been girls, raising them would have come as second nature to her. She would have shown her daughters how to become women, sharing a common language with familiar experiences and gestures. But not fully understanding the whats and the why' of the male world meant Mrs. Turner often second-guessed herself. Like when Jamie, her oldest son, needed an athletic support—better known as a jock strap—for gym, Mrs. Turner was mystified and embarrassed when the store clerk asked what size.

But her lack of knowledge about the male world did not stop her from attempting to negotiate it. No, it just motivated her all the more to conquer it. Many times she was too proud to ask her husband questions about males and therefore the boys suffered through some of her experimentation. Yet her biggest fears were the unknowns that lurked outside of the house. Being a parent of four African American males during a time when being black and male could be hazardous to your health was overwhelming for her. Eventually, Mrs. Turner developed her own way of maneuvering the male world of her family while protecting her sons from forces that she perceived as wanting to destroy them. Silently, she would pray every night for her sons' safety. Only after they were all safely asleep did Mrs. Turner allow herself to rest.

Still smiling at the thought of her sons, Mrs. Turner suddenly remembers that tomorrow is planting day for the garden. Planting day meant that all of her boys would be home to work in the garden and visit their dear old mother. *My boys are coming home. I guess I need to get up and get started preparing some food for them because tomorrow will be here before I know it.*

"Asshole!" yells Daniel as he veers sharply to the right after being cut off by a taxi. Visibly upset, Daniel steers his old, yellow, ten-speed Schwinn off the street onto the sidewalk and stops. With sweat pouring down his face and his thirty-eight-year-old heart pounding like a bass drum, Daniel attempts to calm himself down.

Philly drivers suck, especially the cab drivers, he thinks.

Riding a bike in Philly is no joke—with the busses, inconsiderate drivers, and trucks, not to mention the narrow streets and those rim-bending cobblestones. After a couple of deep breaths to compose himself, Daniel glances around at where he has stopped. It was one of those early spring mornings in May, a little cool but ideal weather for bike riding. The trees were proudly displaying their spring foliage. Many of the lawns needed mowing since the spring rains had produced new growth. Tulips, lilies, and rose buds were struggling to make their appearance in some of the flowerbeds. This time of the year reminds Daniel of being at home working in the family garden. He truly enjoys spring since it signaled the beginning of planting season. Tomorrow he is traveling home to help plant the family garden. Something about the smell of moist soil makes Daniel feel whole.

For as long as he could remember, Daniel's family had had gardens—big ones and small ones. His parents are from down south, Georgia born and bred. He can recall his father's stories of having to pick cotton, beans, and watermelons in the hot summer sun for little to nothing. His mother's family members were sharecroppers too, but she never talked that much about her childhood experiences. If you didn't know any better, you would think she had lived up north all of her life.

Although his parents did not want the sharecropping life for their children, they understood there were life lessons to be learned from interacting with mother earth. Having been raised poor but proud, his parents attempted to use the garden to instill in their children the simple values gathered from their own lives. One of his father's favorite sayings was "In them fields, boys, there is always a lesson to be learned." As a child, Daniel and his siblings entered garden competitions at school, often winning blue ribbons. Yes, having a green thumb was a badge of honor in the Turner household. Although planting season generally begins earlier in some places, Cleveland, Ohio, is one of those midwestern cities known for long winters and short springs. To be sure that it will no longer snow and the plants will have enough time to mature for fall harvest, planting time is usually pushed to Memorial Day weekend.

Yea, this is a good day to be in a garden, Daniel thinks as he looks around. He notices that the street he has stopped on is all row homes—an east coast solution for supplying cheap houses to a large population of people in a city with very little space. They are similar in design and built next to each other for the length of the street. Philadelphia is filled with them. The idea of living that close to someone in that similar of a house was quite distasteful to Daniel. After living in Philly for the past ten years, Daniel had yet to develop a tolerance for one of the realities of the east coast: too many people in too little space. Daniel removes his helmet, wipes the sweat from his face, and then places his helmet back on. He adjusts the straps, remounts his bike, and starts pedaling down the street. In the distance, Daniel hears gunshots, or maybe it was just a car backfiring. The sounds of the city return Daniel to reality.

As part of his daily routine, he stops at Sister Juanita's newspaper stand on the corner of Chew and Washington. Sister Nita, as she likes to be called, is known for her southern drawl, and rumor has it, for burying three husbands. Though Sister Nita has been living in Philadelphia for the last twenty years, when she talks, it sounds like she never left her doublewide trailer in the backwoods of South Carolina. Sister Nita can be an intellectual, a flirt, or a gossip, depending on the time of day and with whom she is talking. Her newsstand is really a mini store, meeting place, and coffee shop all combined in one. At Sister Nita's, you can buy coffee, tea, or juice along with the usual complement of newspapers and magazines while hearing the latest news on the street.

As usual, there was a small gathering of souls at the newsstand discussing the happenings of the day. Daniel parks his bike and wanders up to the newsstand. He waves to the regulars and greets Sister Nita. This morning, Sister Nita seems to be in a talkative, flirtatious mood, which could be problematic if you were in a hurry to get to work.

"Good morning, Sister Nita."
"Morning, teach. You married yet?"
"No, ma'am."
"Who you calling ma'am?. Are you calling me old?"
"No, ma'am. I mean, no, Sister Nita. But any day now …"

"What you waiting for? If I wasn't already married, you would be mine. And you got a job too. That just like icing on the cake."

"Thanks for the compliment, I guess. Can I have my usual? My students are waiting. Make sure my jelly donut is fresh."

Daniel's usual consisted of a small black coffee, a jelly donut, and the *New York Times*. Not a big coffee drinker, Daniel discovered early in his work life that coffee, rather than orange juice, was a good buy on his salary. Since Sister Nita's coffee can be bitter at times, buying a jelly donut is necessary to counteract its unique taste. Buying the less expensive drink also allows him to justify purchasing the *New York Times*, which cost fifty cents more than the daily city paper. In Daniel's lofty opinion, the information in the *Times* was superior to local newspapers and worthy of the additional cost.

"Are you questioning my integrity, young man?"

"No, ma'am. I mean Sister Nita. Just the freshness of your donuts."

Attempting to end the conversation before Sister Nita became longwinded on the relationship of integrity and freshness, Daniel tries to change the subject by asking Sister Nita about her least favorite subject: Philadelphia's Major League Baseball team, the Phillies. So how about them Phillies?"

"They suck, as always. They can't pitch, or hit. Here, take your order and get your little smart ass to school. What do you know about baseball anyway?"

Works like a charm, thinks Daniel.

With a grin on his face, he pays for his order and places it in the basket attached to his handlebars. Attempting to avoid another near-death situation and to not spill his coffee, Daniel merges cautiously into oncoming traffic. Unfortunately, he doesn't see the blue car approaching him. Hearing the car's horn, he quickly pulls his brakes, discovering that fresh coffee can be very hot when spilled on oneself.

His scream of pain draws the attention of Sister Nita and the regulars who were hanging around.

"Hey, teach!" yells Sister Nita, trying not to laugh. "You all right? You almost killed yourself."

"Yea," says Daniel, "I just did not see the car. Spilled some coffee on my pants."

"Do you always scream so loud when you are excited?" asks Sister Nita, laughing.

Not waiting for the answer, four or five of the regulars joined Sister Nita in a round of laughter.

Embarrassed but not defeated, Daniel answers, "Wouldn't you like to know?"

Smoke, one of the regulars, hollers out, "Make sure you look both ways before you cross the street, teach. Don't want you to spill your coffee again."

Tired of being the butt of their jokes, Daniel nods to the group while silently cursing them out. He gets back on his bike and rides to work with his coffee-stained pants and half-cup of coffee.

As he rides away, he can still hear them laughing and making jokes about him. *Thank God it's Friday,* thinks Daniel. *Maybe by Monday they will have forgotten what happened and the jokes could be about someone else.* He doubts it, though. Regulars like Smoke, a dark-skinned former fireman, thus his name, just waits for moments like these to make their day.

Daniel rides the remaining distance to work without incident. By the time he arrives at the K. Maxwell Middle School, he's in a better mood. It's Friday, and he only has to teach four classes instead of his usual six-class load. Since the age of eight, Daniel had always wanted to be a gym teacher. Even at that early age, Daniel concluded that what Mr. Towers—his elementary gym teacher—did looked more like play than work. Daniel knew it was the job for him. Although his family attempted to persuade him to go into other professions, such as medicine or law, Daniel never wavered from his first love. As he once told one of his teaching colleagues, "Who else can wear sweats to work, be involved in sports all day, work only 183 days a year, and still get paid as much as everyone else in teaching? The answer, of course, is the gym teacher."

CHAPTER 2

Helena Mae Turner

I was born Helena Mae Robinson, but strangely I did not know my last name until I was eight years old. Reason being that nobody ever called me by it until my first day of school. Back when I was growing up, a child did not have to attend school until they were eight years old. Mrs. Aspinwall, my first, second, third, and fourth grade teacher, was the first person who I can remember calling me by my whole name. She was one of the nicest white women I had ever met. Rumor had it that she was partial to colored folks because her father was colored, but that was just rumor. On the first day of school, while taking attendance, she called the name "Helena Mae Robinson." Well, I just sat there at my desk looking around to see who had the same first name as me. Of course, none of my thirty-five classmates answered. I think someone pointed at me. Mrs. Aspinwall looked in my direction and said, "Ain't that your name, child? Don't you know your own name?"

"Yes, ma'am, that's my name," I said as I looked up innocently. "Just did not know that Robinson was part of it."

She just shook her head and smiled. I do not know if it was the simple manner in which I responded to her or what, but something occurred in this brief interaction that caused her to look favorably upon me. From that day on, until the fifth grade when I transferred to that mean cross-eyed Mrs. Ross' classroom, I was the teacher's pet and loved every minute of it.

But seriously, I think that my family has a problem with this name thing. Not only did I not know what my last name was, I was a little confused about my first name too. I was named after my grandmother, whose name is Helena. So when I was born, my family called me Little Helena, but for some reason, the name did not stick so they started calling me Helen. Why the name Helen? I do not know. Maybe they thought it would be short for Helena. But I didn't know the truth until my grandmother said to me one day, "Child, your name is not Helen. Your name is Helena."

Did I find out the truth? I realized that in my family we have a thing about being someone who you are not. Truly, I did not know my name was Helena until I was four years old and did not know my last name until I was eight years old. But I guess you have to be named something for someone to notice you.

The town that I escaped from was called Clairville, Georgia. It could have been named Hell if the name had not already been taken. It was twenty-five miles from anything and everything. Understand Clairville was not a big town. It was nothing but a couple of dry-good stores, two or three gin joints, a food market, and a few other businesses. The town maintained a colored section and a white section. The town's motto was "Down here we still do it the old-fashioned way." It was a place where time had stood still, such that the Confederate flag still flew over the county courthouse proudly, and many still thought that the South had won the "Big War," as they called it down there.

There were two schools in town, one for the whites and one for the colored. The school that I attended was John Bellwood Day School for the Colored, on the south side of town. The school was located in a former barn. The cows might have been gone, but their smell remained—a reminder that you were in a barn. Ruby Mae Parker, Aunt May's neighbor, told my mama the school was named after John Bellwood, a Confederate general who was born in Clairville. I do not know if he won any battles or killed any Yankees; all I know is what Ruby Parker told Mama, who then told me.

The Bellwood teaching staff consisted of three white teachers and one colored aide. They taught about one hundred of us children from October to April, and our ages ranged from eight to sixteen years old. Not surprisingly, a lot of the children looked forward to when school was in session, but not for educational reasons. Going to school was an escape from working alongside their parents in the fields. I guess I was a little different because I did not dislike school, but I did not look forward to it either. I enjoyed working in the fields. Although the work was hard, hot, and there were no bathroom facilities, I would rather work outside instead of being cooped up in a hot schoolroom. Okay, maybe I did not like the work, but I enjoyed what the work gave me, something that I craved for more than anything else: positive attention from adults. So being one of the few kids that wanted to go work in the fields made me special, which in turn brought me the attention from adults that I desired. I loved to hear them say, "Look at that Helena work. Her Mama must be proud of her. Sammy boy, that lazy bastard of mine, is scared of hard work, but not that Helena."

Those words made me work harder, because now there was an expectation and I did not want to disappoint anyone, especially my parents.

Working in the fields did have other benefits though, like all there was to learn out there. Through planting and harvesting, the fields became my classroom outside of school. While the fields supplied the naturalistic laboratory for observation of life sciences, the field workers were my instructors, unknowingly teaching me their versions of history, sociology, and psychology. During our too few and too short work breaks, there was always some type of discussion going about the Big War, Joe Louis, or the craziness of white folks. These discussions were generally between Nate, the half-black, half-Cherokee foreman, and one of the workers. Old Yalla, a name the field workers called Nate behind his back because of his light-skinned complexion, was a self-made know-it-all who enjoyed spouting his views of the world to all who would listen. His complexion and job status gave him a perceived superiority, which infuriated most of the workers to the point that the discussions were not just discussions. Oh no, the discussions became the verbal battlefield for the haves against the have-nots. Yes, I would be right there sitting in my place of honor on the floor by Mama watching Old Yalla battle it out with anyone willing to state an opposing position. And on any given day, there were several takers. As a rule, children were not allowed to be around when grown folk discussed anything, but remember I was special.

Amazingly, I learned a lot of good stuff during those discussions. Like the ability to express your ideas without getting upset with your opponent, no matter what they said about you. People calling your ideas stupid, silly, and dumb, and you not fighting back—now that was an education. On the other hand, my formal education was a bad joke with bad teachers, bad instruction, and a bad building that leaked when it rained, but we just did not know any better. We thought that our perceived good education would lead us out of the fields that our parents toiled in year after year. So we were eager and determined, but just not smart enough to understand the ways of the world.

Education did open our eyes so that we could see life differently, but it was that very difference that scared many of my classmates right back to those fields, working beside their parents for the rest of their lives.

The house that I lived in was constructed sometime before Christ. It had five rooms, no running water, and sat in the middle of the vegetable fields. Along with Grandma Helena, Daddy, Mama, and my brother Jimmy, who was five years older than me, we all resided in this shack we called home. With the water well, the chicken coop, and the occasional green snake crawling through the bedroom, living there was quite a natural experience. The house and the fields belonged to our landlord, and my family's only employer in our American existence, the Tucker family.

My family had worked in the Tuckers' fields since my great great grandparents had come unwillingly from Africa as slaves. When I asked about our unique living situation, my grandma Helena told me that when slavery was officially over, it took up another form, and that was why we lived in the middle of the fields with no running water.

I learned at an early age that your perception can become your reality. For example, if you asked Mr. Tucker, he would say that in those fields were planted green beans, peas, greens, watermelons, and cotton. But my Aunt May, my mother's oldest sister who lived down the road, would tell you that Mr. Tucker was wrong. There was far more in those fields than simple vegetables and cotton. She said Mr. Tucker only looks with his natural eyes and therefore he sees what he sees. To understand what is occurring in those fields, Aunt May said that you must look with your soul. Since Mr. Tucker was a white man, he ain't got no soul and thus was blind to the happenings in the field.

Some people might describe Aunt May as being a strange woman because she talked to plants and wore a rabbit foot around her neck and an occasional feather in her hair. Although the unique manner in which Aunt May expressed herself made many people disregard what she said, it was her strangeness that drew me closer to her.

When I was a little girl, Aunt May told me that those fields were magical because spirits lived in them, and simple ole me believed her. That belief ignited my connection to the fields. During the summers before I was enrolled in school, I would go out in the fields to look for signs of the spirits, but never found any. Grandma Helena told me if I did not stay out of those fields so early in the morning something was going to get me, and it may not be human. I did not know if Grandma Helena and Mama believed in the spirits, but I know that they never talked against them.

Aunt May told me that if you listen very carefully at night, you could hear the souls of the slaves in the fields as they gathered to sing songs and play their drums. Well, Aunt May must have good hearing, because the only things that I ever heard were owls, crickets, frogs, and an occasional stray dog howling. But Aunt May must have heard something, because whenever there was a full moon, she would be in our backyard sitting near that mulberry tree just a-moaning and rocking. It was like she was in tune to something. It was spooky.

At first, Aunt May ignored me. Anytime I would inquire about anything, she would shoo me away. But in time, I wore her down with questions about this and that, so she began telling about the plants and herbs that grew in the fields. She showed me which herbs to use to calm an upset stomach, break a fever, and get rid of moldy smells. As our talks moved on to other things, they became longer and more in-depth, while at the same time they began scaring the shit out of me. I did not want to know about all the spirits that lived in the fields. I was just interested in the plants, herbs, and maybe a couple of insects. Generally, Aunt May overlooked my frightened stares while she told me what she thought I needed to know. These talks typically took place after dinner under the mulberry tree in the backyard. The tree was shady and it looked out on the western section of Mr. Tucker's empire—a very scenic view.

One day, while she sat watching the sun set on the cotton fields, Aunt May closed her eyes and said to me in a deep, dark voice—one that I had never heard before—"The most important knowledge to have is the ability to call on the spirits."

In my terrified state I asked, "Why?"

Aunt May smiled and stated simply, "For help and strength."

For the next five nights, right after sunset, she taught me the hows and whys of calling on the spirits, and those lessons changed my life.

Besides learning about roots, herbs, and calling on the spirits, Aunt May taught me that there are reasons why I was so connected to the fields. From a spiritual point of view, the connection was the natural occurrence of the seasons. No matter how difficult my life seemed as a child, the seasonal nature of the fields gave me hope that there was a better time coming. The very act of planting is based on hope. The farmer hopes for a good harvest. Although rain may be slow coming, hope remains. During the winter season, life is somewhat dormant, but hope remains for the spring.

Those fields had another special connection with me. According to Grandma Helena, I was born in the fields while my mama was picking beans. She said that Mama was still working in the fields when she was nine months pregnant with me. Grandma Helena was working behind her and she heard Mama holler, and the next thing she knew, Mama was showing her a baldheaded baby girl and saying, "Isn't she cute?" I never found out if that was a true story or not, but I guess you have to be born somewhere.

There were two events that truly characterized my childhood: my first day of school and the year my brother was killed. Jimmy's murder happened in April of 1947; we had just started back in the fields and were looking forward to a good year. Daddy said Mr. Tucker told him if the farm had a profitable harvest, we might be able to get the septic tank that he had promised us. So there were possibilities in the air—until a look, a disagreement, and one bullet sucked all the hope out of my family. I do not know what my older brother did to get himself murdered. Aunt May said that the Klan killed Jimmy because he talked back to a white man. My mama said that Jimmy was in the wrong place at the wrong time, but Daddy never said a mumbling word about it. To my recollection, there was no investigation, and no one was ever charged with the murder of my brother.

Although his death did not cause white people to stop and take notice, Jimmy's murder had a profound effect on my parents. The day after my brother's funeral, Daddy stopped doing his usual habit of sitting out front of the shack after work, talking to whoever walked by. He just quietly disconnected himself from those around him. He sat in the back under the old mulberry tree, just rocking with his head down, saying nothing to nobody, not even to Aunt May. Daddy left the rocking chair under the mulberry tree only to sleep and to relieve himself. Mama brought all of his meals out there, setting them on the little picnic table that I constructed. Not surprisingly, he hardly ate anything; Daddy's mind was somewhere else.

Seeing that his son had been murdered, his actions appeared to be reasonable. But when the mourning time was up, not only had Daddy stopped talking to people, he didn't return to work either. You need to understand Daddy had never missed a day's work in his life. Even when Mr. Tucker sent Old Yalla to talk to Daddy about coming back to work, Daddy said nothing and continued to sit under out under that tree. Four weeks after Jimmy was buried, Aunt May found Daddy dead in the rocking chair under the mulberry tree. She was shaken by her discovery, especially because during the last full moon, the spirits had told her that someone in the family would die because of a broken heart.

Aunt May did not know if it was the personal sorrow of having his only male child killed or the inability to avenge his death, but Jimmy's murder sucked all the joy out of my father. I soon understood that Jimmy was more than a son to my father. He represented a better tomorrow for my daddy. Because of Jimmy, my father worked as a sharecropper his entire adult life and still did not having his own pot to piss in. Yes, Jimmy was the reason he allowed himself to be treated like a pack mule, for smiling when he wanted to cry, for being passive when assertiveness was the natural response. To my father, Jimmy represented revenge for the 130 years we Robinsons toiled in the Tuckers' fields underpaid, disrespected, and made to feel invisible. All the hope that he had for tomorrow left him when Jimmy got murdered. With hope, there is always a reason to live. No Jimmy, no hope. When there is no hope, people die.

Surprisingly, during this time in my life, I learned a lot from my parents. My daddy taught me that sorrow is very personal and it affects each individual differently. No matter how much a person tells you that they understand your situation, they do not. Just like how the meaning of words does not lie in the word itself but in the person who says them, sorrow also has that type of personal interpretation that is colored by an individual's life experiences. Consequently, the sorrow produced by Jimmy's death for my father was different than my mother's or my aunt's. His sorrow was far more entrenched than mine was, and his was inaccessible to anyone but himself. In the end, sorrow became his companion in death. From my mama, I learned that a parent's greatest gift is to give life, and a parent's greatest weakness is not being able to protect that gift. When a woman is pregnant for the first time, she looks forward to the baby coming, but what she does not realize is that the only time she can protect her baby is when it's in her womb. As soon as the baby is born, she has to been concerned with its safety for the rest of her life. This truth would come to be the major challenge in my own life—attempting to protect the gift.

Six months after my father was buried, my mama began to break down. The effects of two broken hearts and the loss of hope had finally started to show in her. There were early signs of her losing touch, which everyone who lived in our condition would call normal, like the crying at night and talking aloud to herself in her bedroom. But when those behaviors seeped into the daytime hours, that's when it began to affect her day-to-day activities. You need to understand that my mama always treated her men folks like royalty. She believed that since white men had an inherited inferiority complex and no soul, they had a tendency to hold black men back, so it was her job to lift her men up. Mama believed, because my father believed, that their firstborn male child would lead the family to the promised land. She was more devastated over Daddy's death than my brother's. Like my father had invested his hope in my brother, my mother had invested hers in my father, and now she was bankrupt. But unlike my father, my mother's tolerance for being mistreated and dealing in foolishness had always been low. Often she had to be told by Daddy to hold her tongue while witnessing incidents that she perceived as unfair. But now that her bridle was gone, along with her hope, it was a different day for Mama. Once she started talking aloud to herself during the day, everything and anything came out of her mouth.

All was well until one fateful day in July. Early that morning while conducting my daily inspection of the fields near our house, I found a dead crow under the mulberry tree. From my many talks with Aunt May, I knew that a dead crow symbolizes something, but for the life of me, I could not remember what. Not liking to be overwhelmed with the things of life, I dismissed the dead crow to focus on the day at hand. Anyway, I knew I would be seeing Aunt May later so I would ask her then, understanding that she would fuss at me about not remembering anything.

During that day at work, Old Yalla assigned me the job of filling the field hands' water buckets. Although the buckets were heavy to carry, the cool water splashing on my skin was refreshing, so the job did have some rewards. Mama and Aunt May were picking beans in the field ahead of me. The next thing I know, Old Yalla went over to Mama to say something to her that she did not like. Astonishingly, when asked, Aunt May cannot recall what he said to my mama, but we all can remember what happened next. Mama began talking to herself aloud, calling Old Yalla every name under the sun.

Well, you know Old Yalla did not like that at all. He yelled at my mother, "Woman, I do not know what is the matter, but you are messing with the right nigger now."

She never looked in his direction; she just kept cussing him out while picking beans. It was quite a sight, my mama, all eighty-eight pounds of her, cussing so loud that it could be heard down on the road, with six-foot-four Old Yalla towering over her, but she was paying him no mind. While some of the workers told Old Yalla to leave my mama alone because she was not right, others egged him on, saying, "What kind of a man are you, being cussed out by a woman who is paying you no attention?" The more she ignored him, the angrier he became.

Well, the situation might have resolved itself since it was the end of the day, but Old Yalla made a fateful mistake. He said something negative about my father. What he said was not important, but that he said something like that at all was unthinkable. A hush went over the gathering and it was like you could hear a pin drop. Mama stopped picking beans and slowly stood up, looking in Old Yalla's direction. Her facial expression was one of disbelief, pain, and hurt. Something snapped, and then Mama rushed faster than I had ever seen her move before toward Old Yalla, shouting, "You said what about my husband? I will beat all the yellow off of you, you sorry-ass half-bred!"

Old Yalla, taken off guard by Mama's behavior, instinctively began to back up. Looking for a way out to save face, he yelled, "What's the matter with you? You crazy, woman?"

"I'm going to show you who's crazy!" Mama shouted back.

But before she could make good on her promise to Old Yalla, she fell dead, right there in the field.

It was the damnedest thing. One moment she was running headstrong toward Old Yalla, full of hate and with intentions of wringing his neck, and the next moment, she was lying on the ground among the bean plants, lifeless and still.

I ran to her side, screaming, "Mama!" at the top of my lungs. But to no avail. She could not hear me; she was already dead.

Sitting there in the fields and crying with my mother in my arms, I felt all alone, even though the workers in the fields had crowded around me. Then it came to me: a dead crow means that a loved one's death is near. With that realization, I cried even louder.

My cries of sorrow must have struck a nerve, that nerve that indicates a person is suffering pure pain, because even old man Tucker came a-running to see what had happened. Aunt May just held me silently in that bean field until I could not cry anymore. This was the first time I heard them. At first, it sounded like the wind was whistling, but the more I listened, the more it sounded like someone far off was singing. Someone who knew the pain of living and the relief of dying. Their voices were getting closer and clearer. Their songs were moving but at the same time joyous. I cannot really explain it, other than to say I heard them. I do not know if anyone else experienced their presence, but the souls of the slaves returned to the fields that day. I was not focused on anything else but those voices. They had come in response to the grief-stricken cries of a child who had lost her mother, ringing out over the fields. They appeared not as spectators of a tragic event, like humans, but for the purpose of celebrating the life of the fallen soul. They came to sing the soul of my mother home, and I heard them as I lay in that bean field.

Yes, I heard them singing, "Swing low, sweet chariot coming for to carry me home. Swing low, sweet chariot coming forth to carry me home …"

Thinking back to the deaths of my parents, it should have been Mama to be the first to go. She was never that healthy, just skin and bones. Those fields had sucked all the life out of her. But it was not her way to upstage her man. To die before her husband would be taking his glory, and this was unheard of by my mama. She did not want him to mourn for two deaths, so she waited. Once the man she had invested all her hope in was gone, it was not possible to hurt her anymore. She died when he died, and we just did not know it. Those who hold on to hope generally die with that hope—thus the story of my parents.

During the year of sorrow, as my aunt May labeled it, Grandma Helena and I took a trip up north to visit her oldest daughter, Caretta, or Aunt Caretta to me. That trip changed my life.

I did not know a lot about my aunt; she left the south when I was a baby and married a well-to-do college man. Mama always talked fondly of her big sister, but strangely, never went to visit her. Aunt Caretta would come down south for a week in the winter and stay with Aunt May, her youngest sister. She could not stay with us because we had no room. My aunt and I were not close, so I was surprised when she invited Grandma Helena and me to visit her in Cleveland, Ohio.

When I heard the news, I squealed like a pig caught in the fence. I was a sixteen-year-old country bumpkin who had never traveled outside of the county, let alone to another state. As happy as I was, in contrast, Grandma Helena was reserved. To my knowledge, my grandmother had never visited her eldest child, always giving excuses about going the next year.

I guess next year finally caught up with her. So we took the Jim Crow bus from Clairville to Atlanta. In Atlanta, we sat again in the Jim

Crow section of the Greyhound until we got to Ohio, where we were allowed to sit anywhere our heart desired. So twenty-six hours, eight pieces of fried chicken, three cans of potted meat, two soda pops, and a packet of crackers later, we arrived at the Greyhound Bus station in Cleveland. It was 6:30 in the morning, and hope had returned.

CHAPTER 3

Sun's Up

It is 5:30 a.m., early Saturday morning. Mrs. Turner is again waiting patiently for the sun to arrive. She often awakens early on Saturday morning, being as quiet as a mouse as to not wake the family. This is Mrs. Turner's time to set her world in order, a world that has become a lot lonelier without her husband, who died suddenly two years ago. The thought of being without her soul mate often brings tears to Mrs. Turner's eyes.

Although never viewed as the perfect couple, Mr. and Mrs. Turner worked together like a well-oiled machine. His job, which he took very seriously, was to earn enough money to meet his family's needs. Conversely, Mrs. Turner's job was to raise their boys and manage the household. Both excelled in their duties. Mr. Turner worked as a factory worker in the Acme plant on the west side of Cleveland. Although viewed by his neighbors as a quiet man, there was no doubt in the Turner household that Mr. Turner was in charge. When asked why he was so quiet by one of his sons, he replied, "The most powerful thing in the universe is the sun. Without it there would be no life, but when it rises in the morning or sets at night, it does not make a sound. Just view me as being the sun of this household."

Born in the south in the 1920s, Mr. Turner grew up with a love for family and baseball. Prior to serving in World War II, Mr. Turner had played baseball as a catcher in the Negro League. In the late

1940s, after being discharged from the army, he joined the Great Black Migration out of the south and settled in Cleveland, Ohio. Three years later, he met and married Ms. Helena Robinson. From this union would come four sons: Jamie, Daniel, Willie, and Rob Jr.

Mr. Turner demonstrated love for his family by providing for their needs, even when money was short. His sons, whom he affectionately called "the boys," were what motivated him to spend thirty years of his life working for the Acme Company as a crane operator. When work was plentiful, Mr. Turner would work ten hours a day, seven days a week.

In between work and raising their sons, Mr. and Mrs. Turner experienced the ups and downs of life. Many of the good, thoughtful times for Mr. and Mrs. Turner took place early in the morning on the porch. This was the time that the two of them would share, sitting on the porch drinking coffee, waiting for the sun to come up. *He was a good man,* thought Mrs. Turner. *A very good man.*

The sun, accompanied by its morning symphony, finally arrived, and Mrs. Turner looked out in the direction of the garden. Although there was nothing to see because nothing had been planted, it did not stop her from imagining how the garden would look at harvest time. She was having a moment, visualizing the garden in full harvest. Mrs. Turner saw the garden as more than an assortment of vegetables. She saw it as an extension of herself, a part of herself that was so pure and wonderful that she wanted to share it with her family. The garden is all that Mrs. Turner talks about all winter. Yes, there were Christmas and New Years, birthdays and wedding anniversaries, but the garden always stayed in the forefront of Mrs. Turner's mind.

The garden is a large plot of land located across the street from the Turners' home. Before it became the family garden, a two-story apartment building occupied the lot. The Fraziers, Washingtons, and Harrisons are some of the families that had resided in that apartment building. Over the years, because of a lack of maintenance, the apartment building had fallen into disrepair. It was eventually condemned by the city, knocked down, and the land was cleared.

Unable to locate the owner of the property, the city land bank bought it and attempted to sell the site to homeowners in the neighborhood. The first family asked was the Turners, and a purchase price of six hundred dollars was proposed by the city. Mr. Turner considered it a fair price and agreed. Soon thereafter, Mr. Turner called two of his four sons and requested two hundred dollars from each of them to help purchase the plot, which he promptly received. The next spring, the land was plowed, seeds were planted, and the garden was born.

Mrs. Turner's interest in gardening began when she was just a little girl in the south. Being raised poor and black in the rural south in the 1930s was not an easy existence. Like the rest of her family, Mrs. Turner's first work experience was in the fields. She spent many a day picking beans, gathering peas, chopping cotton, and harvesting melons. During those days, no one was too young to work in the fields. She can remember at the age of six or seven getting water for her mother and grandmother as they worked the fields. Yes, those were the days—days that Mrs. Turner tries to forget. They were filled with so much death and personal trauma that Mrs. Turner had repressed most of her memories of her home life. Any attempt made by someone to ask her about her childhood was met with silence and a quick change of subject. Somehow, Mrs. Turner was able to separate her love for nature from her past life. She had always been amazed how such a little thing like a seed could bring forth such a wonderful abundance of life. That childlike amazement remained with Mrs. Turner throughout her life and continued to produce the same sense of wonder within her every spring.

"Yes," says Mrs. Turner, "it's going to be a beautiful garden this year."

She walks down the porch steps—looking down, she notices that they need to be repainted—and opens the gate that leads to the garden. Looking out to what will be the garden come spring, Mrs. Turner sees the remains of last year's cut off cabbage stumps in a trash can, tossed there by the city workers who came out yesterday with a tractor to till the soil. Her placid feelings of calm are replaced by rage when she looks at the mulberry tree that is planted in the garden. It was planted there by Daniel a long time ago, and now it is huge and has become a home for those damn noisy birds. *This will be your last year; no longer will you bother me,* thought Mrs. Turner. She looked around and said aloud, "Those boys, those sorry-ass, good-for-nothing boys, I'll be damned. They have yet to do anything to that garden. How in the hell do they think that all of those seeds are going to get planted? By me? Don't they know that today is planting day? Oh, I wish Daniel lived here instead of in Philadelphia. The garden would be ready for planting if he was here. Those sorry bastards. Wait until I talk to them."

Her disappointment about her sons' lack of effort in the garden is offset by the love that she possesses for them. If it is true that sons are a woman's pride and measure, then the Turner boys are Mrs. Turner's pride and joy. Mrs. Turner never wanted a girl; all she ever desired was to have boys—lots of boys. She believed that a girl would give away her love foolishly to the first man who looked her way, but a boy's first love is to his mother and there it would remain forever, if it was up to her.

Her need to be loved caused her to jealously guard her precious relationships with her sons from any interloper, male or female. Initially, Mrs. Turner was unaware of her covetous behavior and attempted to rationalize it by making statements like "So and so, I forget their name, called you and they must not have wanted anything, because if they did, they would have called back," after giving a message two days late to her oldest son. But after her third son, this behavior became less conscious to her and more just a way of life.

Her sons endured their mother's sabotaging behavior toward their female acquaintances in silence with the full knowledge that it was occurring. They knew if they confronted their mother about her behavior, she would deny it and curse them out. Thus, the brothers took it upon themselves to school the next brother in line about their mother's ways. They made certain their female friends seldom visited the house or called. On the rare occasion that one of them did visit, the brothers made sure they warned the female visitor about their mother's potential for cold behavior toward them. Mrs. Turner's "No female is good enough for my boys" attitude did not prevent the boys from having love interests; it just limited her exposure to those interests. This arrangement met Mrs. Turner's approval since it was exactly what she wanted anyway.

As the boys grew older and moved out of the house, Mrs. Turner's influence over them weakened. One by one, she lost her sons to other female interests. It was her contention that those damn girls just wanted to hurt her boys, but the boys did not want to listen to her. She believed that no one but her had the boys' best interest in mind, not even her loving husband. She ruled her home well, but her self-confidence revolved around what she could do for the Turner men. She truly loved her men, but as the years went by, she realized that she needed her family to need her more than she needed them to love her.

The gradual loss of her sons' attention, along with the death of her husband, put Mrs. Turner in a deteriorating emotional state. Unknown to her family, her view of herself had been damaged, causing her to become depressed. Through the garden, however, Mrs. Turner found herself again. It became her new lover, and thus a new reason for living. Although each of the sons had promised their mother they would help prepare the garden for planting, nothing had been done, and today is the Saturday before Memorial Day, the official Turner family planting day. Looking at the unplanted garden with disgust, Mrs. Turner thinks, *I should wake up those sorry-ass bastards.*

Her thoughts propel her into action: she walks back into the house and yells at the top of her lungs to the one son sleeping in the house, after which she calls the other three at their homes. She tells them in the colorful language that she is known for that it would be in their best interests to come by the house this morning to work in the garden.

Jamie sits straight up in the bed when the phone rings. His wife kicks him and mumbles something about answering the phone. Jamie was the oldest son of the Turner clan. He used the good fortune of affirmative action and a master's degree from Central State University to rise up the corporate ladder until he hit the glass ceiling. He is now the director of communication for the ACOLE Corporation. Married but childless, his brothers perceive him as the "mama's boy" of the family.

"The phone? I thought I was dreaming."
"Yea, the phone."
"Are you sure? It's 6:30 in the morning."
"There is goes again. Answer it, damn it. It's for you."

Reluctantly, Jamie picks up the receiver, already knowing who's on the other end and why she's calling.

After a couple of yes-ma'ams, he hangs up the phone and slumps back down in the bed.

Carole asks just one question. "What time does she want you there?"
"9 a.m."
"You are such a good son."

Carole turns back over to get some well-deserved sleep.

At 6:35 in the morning, Rob Jr. is awakened by his mother. Rob Jr., the youngest son, lives in an apartment in downtown Cleveland. He's college educated—and single. After a late night out with his friends, the phone call from his mother is unexpected, and not pleasant. Yea, he knew that he had promised to work in the garden, but things happen, and Mama knew it would get done. The conversation was nothing that he had ever heard before from her, and he knew that his mother meant business. He slowly sits up in bed, looking at the clock and shaking his head.

Why couldn't the phone call have been from Bev? She's my early morning phone caller, not Ma.

For the last eight months, Bev has been Rob Jr.'s sole romantic interest. They enjoy each other's company and intimacy and share a love for a good apple martini. Rob Jr. is scared and stuck. He is scared to tell Bev how he truly feels, which leaves him stuck in a place where he does not want to be. He can remember his father's words reverberating in his head, telling him that a "scared man cannot do anything."

Rob Jr. recalls his phone conversation with Bev the day before. The phone had rung promptly at 6:45 a.m., as it does every weekday morning. Although he had been waiting impatiently for the call, the ring startled him. Rob Jr. let the phone ring twice before answering it; he did not want to appear too anxious. His previous conversation with Bev had not gone well, so he was not sure that she would be calling that morning.

At the end of the second ring, Rob Jr. grabbed the phone like it was the lifeline to his heart. Not surprisingly, Rob Jr.'s attempt to be cool failed, and his voice cracked as he said hello to Bev. Despite his opening jitters, the rest of the conversation proceeded without incident.

As the conversation winded down, Rob Jr. hesitated for a couple seconds, unsure of what to say. It was one of those crossroad moments in a relationship, where your destination depends on that moment. Maybe there were other factors at play, such as the time of the day, not having had his first cup of coffee yet, or the Friday morning blues, that prevented Rob Jr. from sharing his true feelings with Bev. Instead of using the opportunity to reassure his commitment to Bev by saying something like "I love you," Rob Jr. ended with "Have a nice day; I will talk to you later." As soon as the words left his mouth, Rob Jr. knew they were wrong, and why.

Sitting up in his bed, now wide-awake, Rob Jr. reaches for a silver watch on the nightstand. The watch had once belonged to his father. It was an automatic-winding Bulova, one of those types of watches that did not require a battery but automatically rewound itself with the movement of the person's arm. Mr. Turner was proud of that watch;

Rob Jr. could remember his father sitting at the breakfast table and just moving his arm around and around to wind the watch. It was one of the few items of his father's that he chose to keep after his death. In that moment, visions of his father winding the watch flood his consciousness and his eyes well up with tears. A feeling of loneliness overcomes Rob Jr., and he begins to cry aloud uncontrollably.

The crying episode lasts this time for about five minutes, much longer and more intense than the last time. These unannounced spontaneous rise of emotions frighten Rob Jr. because he is unsure of what they mean. He understood where the feelings came from but did not understand why it was happening now, at this moment. There has not been a day since his father's passing that Rob Jr. has not thought of his father. When Rob Jr. received the news of his death, he remembered not knowing how to feel. He had just seen his father; how could he be dead? He was abruptly immersed in a state of shock, which did not allow him to process the emotional condition that was raging within him. Rob Jr. wrote the following passage in his journal.

6/06/2002

When I received the news that my father had passed, I did not know how to feel—I was in a state of "no feelings." I would not say it was shock or denial, just no feelings. The next day, sorrow overcame me, causing me to become very tearful every time I thought of my dad. As far as support, it was less than I expected. One or two female friends attempted to console me, but overall, people were kind, thoughtful, but standoffish. Shoot … I have not seen Que Dog for a couple of days. They did offer support in the way of saying, "I'm praying for you" or "I heard that your father had passed," but little else. I expected more, but soon realized that it would not be forthcoming.

The sense of abandonment that he felt forced him to conclude that it was easy for people to be sympathetic to his situation, but difficult to empathize with him. His loss and need to be comforted was personal. It was not easy for people to communicate to him on that level.

Although he loved his father, Rob Jr. remembers that he did not cry at the funeral. No, he was a Turner man, and crying over loss was something they were taught not to do. His refusal to publicly grieve has troubled Rob Jr. ever since. He could remember crying over losing a silly baseball game, but publicly, he shed no tears over losing his father. Mr. Turner's death had a confusing effect on not only Rob Jr. but also his brothers. Other than the knowledge that their father was dead, none of the brothers had yet to come to terms with how to honor their father's death.

Shortly after 9 a.m., Rob Jr. arrives at his mother's house. His brothers are already there, but not yet working in the garden. They are all sitting on the porch like it is the place to be that morning. The Turners' front porch has an awning that shields it from the morning sun, which made it an ideal place to sit, talk, and watch people. There they sit, Mrs. Turner, Jamie, Willie, and Daniel, talking about something and looking in Rob Jr.'s direction. *Daniel's here? What the heck is he doing here?* thought Rob Jr. *Ma must have called and cussed him out too.*

> "Good morning. What's for breakfast?"
> "About time your lazy ass got here," remarks Mrs. Turner.
> "And a good morning to you too," quips Rob Jr.

Mrs. Turner's tone, demeanor, and colorful speech could be viewed as harsh and unnecessary to an outsider. But for Mrs. Turner, the way she speaks to others, especially the boys, reflects not a lack of love but a fear of loving too much. She would never be told that she babied her boys. No, her boys would develop into what every woman desired in a man if she had her way. If that meant that she had to be a little harder on them than what others thought was necessary—well, that was just too bad.

Chapter 4

Carole

I stretch out in the bed attempting to reposition my body for the nth time after an early morning disturbance. An hour after the call from his mother, Jamie showered, got dressed, gave me a kiss, and ran off to her. He is such a mama's boy.

Jamie's absence made the bed seem like a small, cold, and unconnected place. I curl back up in a little ball and begin rocking and thinking about my life over the last six years. I'm eight months pregnant and not liking any of it. I'm bigger than big, my back hurts, and my feet are constantly swollen. I'm so large that the doctor placed me on bed rest, forcing me to stop working. This little baby girl better hurry up and come, or there is going to be hell to pay. But despite the physical discomforts of my present situation, I would do it all over again. Jamie is an amazing man, with a boatload full of faults, but he is mine. I really love him, and at this moment, I miss him. He means everything to me. I grab his pillow like it was him, bringing it close to me until I can smell him. His scent is still lingering on the pillowcase, causing a smile to appear on my face. I lay there in my oversized T-shirt with my bloated stomach, wondering what time my Mandinka warrior will be back home.

I met Jamie eight years ago while waiting for a train. I was a twenty-nine-year-old recently divorced social worker. After a rocky five-year marriage, I had divorced my cheating husband. Following a long period of self-reflection, I decided to give myself a break from men and used the time to focus on me.

Exempting men from my life was difficult, but necessary. I discovered that I had become too needy for their love, which consequently placed me in a position of weakness. Following that moment of self-discovery, I sought out every "Love Yourself; You Do Not Need A Man" conference I could find. After attending about five of these seminars, ranging in topics from women's health needs to how to be good without a man, I had a revelation. First of all, some of the information was just wrong. The speakers frequently talked about how we as women should love ourselves before seeking out a mate to love. But how does that work? How can you love yourself if you have never experienced someone else's love? Who or what experience do I model this love for self after? The truth, I was to find out, is that you cannot love yourself unless you have been loved.

The ability to love is a social phenomenon, not something you can create by yourself. On the other hand, some of the stuff was good. The speakers at the conferences encouraged the attendees to develop a sense of self worth within each of them, which due to past poor models in my life, I required a lot of work on. This was some of the good stuff; I never realized how much of my self-perception of who I was had been shaped by others and not by me. After some time, I realized that my perception of who I was had been formed by mixing some terrible advice from my mother along with the point of view of every man who I had ever dated. The realization that my previous self-worth was a creation of this toxic manifestation first scared me, and then angered me. It took me a while to get used to the changes that I wanted to take place within me.

I was surprised to find out that the women who attended these seminars were professionals with successful careers. Stupidly, I had thought that the successful businesswomen had it all together and would not need any development of self. To the contrary, the conferences were filled with a sea of beautiful women dressed to the

T. If I did not know any better, I would have thought a Coach bag was a required accessory.

The downside of the conferences was that there was no follow-up. After getting you all hyped up and ready to face the world, there was no emotional refilling station available when you ran out of steam. What was needed was some kind of real-world practicum where we could try out these new skills and report back to someone for supervision, something like a life coach. But no, we were like salmon swimming upstream with the new knowledge of what to do, but sometimes too tired or just overwhelmed with the tasks before us to make any true headway in our self-development.

A few of us who were able to put our self first did experience a change within ourselves. It was initially a small and uncomfortable change. Just the thought of putting one's self first was difficult to comprehend, let alone do. But it happened, and I began feeling better about myself. *Look out world. I am no longer your doormat. I'm ready to kick some butt.*

Although I had not been in the company of a man for over two years, romance was not on my agenda when I met Jamie. We took the same train in the morning to work—the 7:52 that stopped at Shaker Square. At first, I did not notice him, or anyone else for that matter. When I'm on the train, I like to be left alone in my own little world. To defend myself from male intruders, I always carried something to read, generally a book. Most guys don't read anything but the sports page, so to disturb a woman while she was reading a book was a social no-no; thus, the book acted as my force field against all interlopers.

It was a Monday morning when Jamie entered my life. I was standing, reading my book, waiting for the train to come, and did not notice that he had walked past me. Jamie later told me that he walked by me, stopped, and backtracked. All I knew is that I heard someone say, "Excuse me, do you like reading *Beloved*?"

I glanced up from my reading and saw this dark-skinned brother with a big smile looking at me.

I replied curtly, "Yea, but it's somewhat confusing. Have you read it?"

But I was thinking, *What does this smiling fool know about* Beloved? *I should have asked if he even reads. It's a book, not a sports page. No, it is a novel. Hey, this is not easy reading either. It's by Toni Morrison. Oh hell, he is still here and is about to open his mouth again.*

Fortunately or unfortunately, Jamie belonged to three book clubs, and one of the book clubs had just finished reading *Beloved*. So for the next couple of minutes, Jamie attempted to explain to me the plot, characterization, and the story line. I stood there impressed, dumbfounded, and in anticipation. I was waiting for those words that spoil the majority of my initial interactions with men. But the train appeared, we said our good-byes, and that was that. As I sat on the train reviewing what had just occurred, a smile crept onto my face while I considered that Jamie might be pleasantly different.

After our first meeting, I began noticing Jamie in the morning if our paths crossed. There was something about him that was different. He did not attempt any of those sorry lines nor did he appear overly interested in me. Jamie was confident yet somewhat timid. I was waiting for the "Baby, baby, please" crap, but it never came. He was refreshing, thoughtful, and not bad-looking. Occasionally, we'd speak to each other, slowly easing our way into small talk. One day we exchanged phone numbers, which led to our first date, and the rest is history.

Since becoming Mrs. Carole Turner five years ago, my life has been quite interesting, to say the least. Beside the many adjustments that a married couple has to make when learning about each other, there are special challenges when you marry a Turner man. One of the biggest challenges I faced was to share my man with another woman. I can remember the first time I met Mrs. Turner. It was at a family cook out seven years ago. I had been dating Jamie for about three months and had never met any of his family.

Anytime I brought up the subject, Jamie would dismiss it by saying, "You are not ready yet."

One day Jamie stated that the family was getting together for the Fourth of July at his parents' house and asked if I would like to go.

"Of course I would love to go," I answered. Then I asked the question that allowed me to receive a taste of what was to come. "Can I bring a dish?"

Jamie just burst out laughing.

"What's so funny?"

Jamie just kept laughing. I can remember yelling at him, not knowing why he was laughing, but I knew it was at my expense.

"Bring something to my mother's house to eat?"
"Yea … What? My food isn't good enough for your family? You eat it."

Jamie, in a sorry attempt not to lose his free homemade meals from my kitchen, tried to explain to me that no one brings any cooked food into his parents' home expecting it to be eaten.

"Why?" I asked.
"Because of her."
"Who?"
"My mother."
"What does your mother have to do with it? Is she scared of a little competition?"

Although I was not at Mrs. Turner's level of cooking accomplishments, I did know my way around the kitchen.

"You need to understand the relationship that food, love, and caregiving has with my mother."

I was then sat down and told that food is equal to love in the Turner family. It was food that bound the family together. Although Jamie had never seen his parents be romantic, he knew that they loved each other. It did not matter what time his father got home, his mother would always get out of bed to feed her man. That, to Jamie, was an expression of true love—the type of love that songs are written about and wars are fought over. Love, to Jamie, was not what you said but how you expressed it. He crazily believed if I brought food to the cookout, it could be interpreted by Mrs. Turner as me thinking she was unable to provide for her family or her food was not good enough for me to eat. I soon learned that by Mrs. Turner's standards, it would be looked upon as disrespectful.

"Bring food of all things to my mama's house—what were you thinking?" stated Jamie, still laughing.

This fool proceeded to explain that this food thing could place him in a terrible situation. Even if my dish looked and smelled wonderful, it would not be in his best interest to compliment it or accept it as an equal to his mother's cooking. Public acceptance by him could mean rejection of his mother, and he was in no position to take that chance yet. We had only been dating for a couple of months, and who knew if it was going to last? It was sadly, or foolishly, understood that choosing me over his mother was not a good risk at this time, which made me aware of the pull that Mrs. Turner had over this son. Now fully conscious of the possible consequences of my actions, I rescinded my offer and awaited my initial meeting of the family with much curiosity.

As the Fourth of July holiday approached, my curiosity about Jamie's family was fading fast. I did not like the idea that I would be on display for people I did not know and, at this moment, did not care to know. Jamie was a nice guy, but not so great that I had to subject myself to the judgment of others.

By the time I arrived to meet Jamie at his parents' house, I was a "sister with an attitude." My much anticipated meeting the family was over quickly, but not without some unexpected drama. The Turners lived on a quiet street on the east side of town. The house was a three-floor single with a big backyard with lots of fruit trees. Across the street from the house was a large fenced-in vegetable garden. It appeared that they had a BBQ in the backyard and people were everywhere, smiling and eating.

I saw Jamie when I pulled up; he was smiling, apparently in a good mood. Jamie opened my door, kissed me gently, and stated that he was glad that I came. He grabbed my hand and walked me up the driveway to the side door of the house. After being introduced to Mr. and Mrs. Bray, Jamie's neighbors, we entered the house.

The interior of the Turners' house had a little too much stuff in it for me. There were pictures all over the walls, giving the house the feel of a museum, a place that you visited but did not stay.

The first members of the family that I was introduced to were two of his brothers, Rob Jr. and Willie. It must have been feeding time at the zoo, because when we were introduced, they never even looked up from their plates, continuing to eat like pigs while taking little notice of me. The feeding frenzy was not only limited to the brothers. There was a scattering of aunts, uncles, and cousins milling around the house and backyard, looking to eat whatever was not nailed down. I do remember Mr. Turner being the only talkative family member of the bunch. When I was introduced to Jamie's father, I instantly knew there was something about him I liked. He appeared interested in me as a person, not as an intruder into the Turners' homeland. His mannerisms were straight country, or as my girlfriend later described him, "straight from 'Bama." His presence allowed me to become more comfortable in what could be depicted as a nonvisitor friendly family.

At the house, even Jamie began acting like his head was screwed on backward. He introduced me to his mother and then quickly disappeared, pretending to hear someone calling his name outside. I looked at him and shook my head.

Mrs. Turner and I exchanged greetings, talked about the weather, and after a couple of minutes, she politely excused herself. I walked off to find that jackass boyfriend of mine with mixed feelings. I was delighted that the first meeting was over but disappointed that I had overreacted to Jamie's ranting about his mother's disposition.

I spied Jamie sitting next to an older, big-hipped woman, who I later learned was his aunt Betty, Mrs. Turner's younger sister. I quietly walked over to them, introduced myself to Aunt Betty, and requested a moment with Jamie.

> With a silly grin on his face, he said, "Well, how did it go?"
> "How did *what* go?"
> "You and my mama. How did it go?"
> "We weren't on a date! But you will not be on one with me much longer if you pull crap like that again."
> "So how did it go?"
> "Jamie, you are an asshole."

And with those words, I saw the man I was falling in love with suddenly become a boy in front of my eyes. I did not know whether to punch him or scream, so I walked away from him. I left him standing there with that same silly grin on his face, shaking his head. I looked around the house and found Mr. and Mrs. Turner sitting next to each other on the porch. I lied and told them about a previous engagement, apologized for leaving so early, and said my good-byes.

As I left the porch, I heard Mrs. Turner asking her husband, "Who was that?"

I wanted to turn around and yell my name to her again and again, saying, "Your future daughter-in-law, Carole Turner," but better judgment prevailed.

My future encounters with Mrs. Turner consisted of a friendly greeting and little else. Although there were no visible signs of fighting, a battle of wits was taking place between Mrs. Turner and me over Jamie's heart. I learned early that she is a master in controlling people's behavior. For example, out of nowhere, Mrs. Turner started addressing me as "baby." At first, this took me by surprise. Attempting to make a good impression on Jamie's mother, I accepted my new name. It was, "Baby, you okay? Baby, you want to sit down? Oh baby, you looked tired." An onlooker might have thought that Mrs. Turner was a very generous and loving soul to address with me with such a term of endearment, but I soon learned better. I was aware that Mrs. Turner did not care for me dating her son and was convinced that this renaming was a method of control. The new name was designed to disconnect me from who I was. Mrs. Turner was attempting to recreate me in her own image, not unlike what the slave masters did to the slaves.

Baby was my new name for about a month—until one day I whispered under my breath to Mrs. Turner that my mother named me Carole and if she called me baby again, I would scream. So just as suddenly as it began, the baby name-calling stopped.

The closer Jamie and I became, the more Mrs. Turner pulled his strings. Yes, she played him just like he was a puppet. I thought that she was going to have a heart attack when we announced our engagement and future wedding plans. The announcement occurred at the end of dinner on a Sunday. Mrs. Turner had begun serving the dessert, homemade peach cobbler. Jamie asked everyone to sit down because he had something to say to the family.

Mrs. Turner, being Mrs. Turner, refused to sit down and demanded that Jamie hurry up because her peach cobbler was getting cold. After Jamie announced to his family our wedding plans, Mrs. Turner mumbled something and slid down into the floor, still holding her peach cobbler. Later, she said it was the new medication that caused her to be dizzy, but I truly believe that the thought of losing one of her precious fine sons was enough to make her heart stop.

This well-disguised theatric caused Jamie to think about canceling the wedding for a moment. He insisted that his mother was not well and needed his attention. I said that she might be sick in the head, but that was about all I saw.

After making sure that his wife was okay, Mr. Turner took his oldest son by the arm and stated that he wanted to talk to him privately. Jamie was torn because he really did not want to leave his mother's side, but he knew his father meant business. Mr. Turner asked everyone, including his wife, to leave the room and go out on the porch. Mrs. Turner's pleas to be included fell on deaf ears.

As we reluctantly left the two of them together to have their man-to-man, I sensed that Jamie was scared—very scared. The tension on the porch was high, which is not unusual when you have two women loving the same man for different reasons. As I sat on the swing, a cool breeze flirted with me in my emotionally drained state and I soon fell asleep.

Twenty minutes later, Jamie poked me in the shoulder, saying it was time to go. We said our good-byes, although his mother was nowhere to be found, and went home. I never asked what was discussed between him and his father on that day. I cannot say that I observed an immediate change in his behavior toward his mother; I believe that he will always be a mama's boy, and I'm okay with that. What I do know is that his behavior toward me changed. He became more interested in me, and he listened and talked to me, which was a big change. So he can keep his old lover just as long as he continues to treat me like his queen.

CHAPTER 5

Review

"Alex, why are you late again for class?"

It's Monday, first period at Kenneth Maxwell Middle School, and Ms. Crook's sixth grade class has been performing soccer drills for the last fifteen minutes.

"I got up late, Mr. Turner."
"Well, find a place on the wall until I can work you into the drill."

Alex Johnson, better known as Alex "Late Shoes" Johnson, had just arrived to Mr. Turner's gym class at his usual time, fifteen minutes late, with a smile on his face. On a normal day, this would have upset Daniel, but after his week spent visiting his mother, Alex's lateness was nothing to be concerned about, relatively speaking.

Daniel's weekend started out just fine. On Saturday, at about 5:30 in the morning, Daniel sped toward the Philadelphia International Airport in the back of a taxi. At 6:25 a.m., Daniel boarded a jet to Cleveland. He noticed that Cleveland was not the most popular destination at 6:25 a.m. The jet seated fifty, but there were only fifteen passengers, counting Daniel. Before the plane took off, Daniel had already fallen asleep. His ability to fall asleep at a moment's notice was one of his greatest gifts.

At 7:45 a.m., right on schedule, the plane touched down at Cleveland Hopkins Airport. Daniel deplaned and walked down the corridor, past security into the waiting area. To the left of security stood a small gathering of people anxiously awaiting the arrival of a loved one. Despite the fact that no one knew he was coming home, Daniel scanned the crowd for a familiar face anyway. He always looked, and was always disappointed. Daniel's need to be independent discouraged him from relying on others; therefore, it was not in his nature to ask someone to meet him at the airport. When asked by family or friends why he did not call someone to pick him up, he would say that he does not like bothering anyone—while secretly suppressing his disappointment that no one took it upon themselves to meet him anyway. Daniel believed that being a man means being responsible for your own needs. His narrow interpretation of manhood caused him to be quite independent, but at the same time, it caused him to be resentful of others for not offering support.

Daniel departed the waiting area for the transportation level and caught the next train into downtown Cleveland. The trip takes about twenty minutes and travels through various neighborhoods. The train ride was as uneventful as the plane trip. Most of the passengers were airport third-shift workers going home after a long night and a too early morning.

Sitting slightly slumped in his seat, Daniel recalled the phone conversation that he had with his mother the day before. It had been 6:30 a.m. Friday morning, her usual time of the day to check in on her sons. He informed his mother, jokingly, that it was quite possible that he would not be able to come home to help her plant the garden this weekend. Unfortunately, Mrs. Turner did not see anything funny in this, and they had an exchange of a couple of choice words. Mrs. Turner then hung up on him. It was her way of saying that she was still the mother and he should play games with his brothers, not her.

After arriving downtown, Daniel hailed a cab, and within fifteen minutes, he was back at the house where he spent his childhood. He paid his fare, retrieved his bag, and turned toward his parents' house.

It looked different now. Daniel could remember the day that they moved into the house thirty years ago. Prior to this house, they rented a three-bedroom apartment in another section of the city. Daniel had not wanted to move out of his old neighborhood but was willing to undertake the personal social sacrifice for the promise of having a backyard. To an eight-year-old who had lived all his life in an apartment, the new house seemed so big and new. But now, years later, it looked smaller and older, not to mention the front steps were in need of painting. On the front porch in the chair that used to be his father's, his mother sat looking right at him.

"I knew that you were coming home, fool!" yelled his mother.

"How did you know that? Are you psychic now?" asked Daniel after running up the steps to give his mother a kiss on the cheek, the only type of touchy-feeling greeting that she accepted.

"Well, I called your ass this morning, and when I did not get an answer, I figured that you were either on your way here or out running. So when you didn't call me back, I knew, because it's planting time."

When Mrs. Turner wanted to get in touch with one of her sons, she employed what came to be known as the early wakeup method. She would call them as early in the morning as possible to wake them up. Pity the son for whatever reason did not answer the phone, because there would be hell to pay.

"Boy, are you losing weight? You need to come home more often so that I can put some fat on those bones."
"Since you figured that I was coming, what's for breakfast?"

Like in many African American families, food in the Turners' house was symbolic for love. Refusing to display positive emotions through the normal channels, Mrs. Turner used food to express her love. It was commonly known in the Turner household that money was never discussed, exchanged, or asked about, but you could have all the food you wanted. If one of the boys were bold or stupid enough to ask either one of their parents for any money, he would get cussed out, laughed at, and talked about. But if one of the boys was hungry, his loving mother would get out of her bed and feed them.

Being back home always created a tidal wave of emotions for Daniel. As he walked through the front door into the living room, Daniel felt that he had been thrust back in time. As soon as the plane landed at Hopkins International Airport, feelings that had been unconscious to Daniel's psyche emerged from their hiding place. These feelings sometimes ambushed him, like they were doing now. Rushing at him unannounced, the feelings bring with them memories, and with the memories come even more feelings. That circular process that takes Daniel temporally back to a time when his world consisted only of his neighborhood, this house, and its inhabitants. Memories, sounds, and smells flood his senses. Daniel comes to expect these feelings when he returns home. He looks at the stairs to the second floor and remembers that as a child, it was his responsibility to clean them every Saturday. The smell of cooked bacon lingered in the air, bringing back memories of having breakfast on the old yellow kitchen table and eating as quickly as he could so that he could ask for a second helping of bacon. Yes, he was back home.

Daniel's breakfast that Saturday morning consisted of bacon, grits, eggs, and coffee, as well as his mother's famous homemade biscuits. If there was one thing that their mother truly excelled in, it was cooking, and biscuits were one of her specialties. Daniel is a good cook in his own right; however, he never has been able to duplicate his mother's biscuits, even with the recipe that she gave him. His poor biscuit making has more to do with not wanting to replace the memories of his mother's biscuits; therefore, unconsciously, he is prevented from being successful.

As Daniel finished his third biscuit topped with jelly, Willie popped his head into the kitchen. Since he was a youngster, Willie has been Daniel's favorite brother. Immature and irresponsible, he could be the poster child for what was wrong with men. Willie was an all-state baseball player at Glenville High School and all-conference centerfielder for Ohio University. During a ski trip, Willie injured his knee and dropped out of school.

With no interest from the pros, Willie got a job with the post office and married his high school sweetheart, Deitra. A situation occurred during their young marriage that even veteran couples would have trouble surviving—and the event caused them to separate. Though still legally married, the emotional distance between the two has grown to the point that a divorce is in the process. When asked about his marriage, Willie always responds with jokes, which probably reflects his difficulty with the situation. For that reason, Daniel purposely did not ask about Deitra, which suited Willie just fine.

Soon after the separation, Willie returned back home, where he resides today. Despite this setback, Willie remains a star in his own mind, which he reminds people of daily while he's walking his mail route. Despite his obvious shortcomings, Willie is silly, funny, and always looking for a good time—characteristics that are endearing to Daniel.

The two brothers wiped their plates clean with their last bits of biscuit, feeling content. They heard a car pull up in the driveway, and the door open and close. Without looking up, Willie said, "There is a disturbance in the force, and unless it's contained, it may destroy everything we hold true."

"I'm not going."
"But you are the oldest."
"And? Let's flip to see who goes."

"Okay."

Pulling out a quarter, Daniel flipped it in the air. "Call it in the air!" Daniel yelled.

"Heads."

Heads it was, and Daniel trudged unwillingly toward the front door to see who the intruder was.

Kneeling down behind the sofa near the front window, a favorite hiding place from his youth, Daniel could see outside without being detected. On the porch sat his mother and oldest brother, Jamie, just laughing and having a good old time, no doubt at someone else's expense. After monitoring the conversation for a couple of minutes and determining that he was not the subject of their ridicule, Daniel decided to join them on the porch to be a part of humiliating whoever it was they were joking about. But a strange thing happened when Daniel open the porch door.

Suddenly, all the laughter stopped and Mrs. Turner and Jamie looked in Daniel's direction like he had interrupted two lovers. Daniel quickly assessed that he had stumbled in on one of those sacred mother and son moments where the two are reconnected back to the time when they were one. These moments confirm the linkage between mother and son while reconnecting their bond. But most of all, these are private moments to be shared between mother and son, not mother, son, and another son.

Sensing that his rejection was justified, Daniel sought to take the high road. He calmly said, "I think I smell something burning in the kitchen," and stepped back into the house.

In the kitchen, Willie was devouring his fourth biscuit with jelly. As he wiped his mouth, Willie muttered, "What's all the fuss about?"

"Jamie and your mother are having a moment."

"They were? But I thought when people have a moment, they be crying and stuff."

"It was not that kind of a moment!"

"Fine. I was just asking."

Then out of nowhere came the sound that you dreaded the most if you were a child in the Turner household: your mother calling your name.

"Daniel."

If Mrs. Turner called your name, it was not a laughing matter. It was an indication that she wanted something from you, and unfortunately, you had no idea what she wanted. Though it did not matter, because whatever she wanted, you would not be able to find. And you would not be able to come up with the correct answer anyway. Projecting as much humility as possible, you could only reply to her calling your name by saying, "Yes, ma'am."

Back in the day, replying, "Yes, ma'am" or "Yes, sir," was a signal to any adult that you, the child, had what they called "home training." But more importantly, it indicated that no matter what the adult asked you to do, they believed in your judgment and that you were willing to accomplish whatever was needed.

As Daniel awaited his fate, Willie whispered to him, "You're in trouble now."
"You and Willie, come here now," Mrs. Turner said.

Although Daniel did not know his fate, he was comforted knowing that he would not be facing it alone. His mind went back to when he was a kid and his mother had asked him to find something in the basement cupboard. Daniel spent the next fifteen minutes looking for something that he could not find but was too scared to tell his mother. Finally she called him, asking what was taking him so long. Daniel stated that he could not find what she asked for downstairs. Then from his mother's mouth came a verbal assault upon him using language so foul that Daniel trembles as he thinks about it now. Adding insult to injury, she came down the steps and easily found the item, which made him feel even smaller than he already felt.

Focusing back on the present, Daniel privately hopes that it will be Willie, and not him, that is asked to go find something for his mother.

Daniel and Willie proceeded to the porch, facing their mother, and said almost in unison, "Yes, ma'am."

Before giving them their marching orders, Mrs. Turner hesitated. A familiar red-and-white car was approaching the house.

That's damn Rob Jr., thought Mrs. Turner.
About time he got here. Now all my boys are home.

CHAPTER 6

Jamie

Shit! I do not believe this, thinks Jamie. *I just told my mother the funniest joke she ever heard, she's laughing, we're having a good time—and that Rob Jr. pulls up. Can't I have some time with my mother without all my attention-seeking brothers hanging around? But I should have known better. It's dig-up-the-garden-day and all of us are due here, on time. My mother's face lit up when Rob Jr. opened his car door. That smile that was once mine now it belonged to him. It just seemed like her demeanor changed. Maybe it's my imagination; it was like she began to glow. I just cannot win.*

As Rob Jr. climbs the stairs, I stand up slowly and warmly embrace him like he was my long-lost brother.

"My baby! My baby!" yells my mother as she greets my younger brother with a much bigger hug than she gave me.

As I stand there, I can remember when it was only Pops, Mama, Daniel, Willie, and me. At that time, each of us had our own room, with mine being the biggest. My bedroom was a reflection of my world and me. There was order, simplicity, and cleanliness. Suspended from the ceiling with fish line was my collection of World War II model planes. Each plane was an exact replica of the full-sized plane, from decals to paint job. The Japanese 6M Zero, the German Messerschmitt BF

109, and P-40 War Hawk were all there. Freud probably would have said that my aggressive feelings for power had been sublimated into a more socially acceptable behavior of model airplane building.

Next to my bedroom window stood my aquarium, or as Daniel called it, my "large fish bowl," in which resided Alicia, a koi goldfish from Japan. Alicia cost me five dollars, and she was worth every penny of it. Next to my nightstand sat my collection of Marvel comic books, which included Spider-man, Iron Man, and the Fantastic Four. I purchased my vast collection by using my birthday and Christmas money and doing odd jobs around the neighborhood. My parents did not believe in giving an allowance.

I can remember taking the issue of allowance to my father. What a mistake. I was ten years old and wanted to buy the latest Spider-man comic. After a lot of thought and preparation, I approached my dad, the breadwinner of the family. I viewed my father as a no-nonsense individual who did not play with children, especially his own. Since I was the oldest, I perceived that my father looked for me to set an example for my younger brothers. What that example was, I was never too clear about, because my father was a man of few words. As I grew up, I came to understand what he wanted, but never what he thought of my actions. That is the reason why I gravitated toward my mother, because she had no problem telling you what she thought of you, or anyone else. But I regress. My dad was sitting at the dining room table and reading the newspaper when I approached him. I said, "Dad, can I have an allowance?"

My father, who had not stopped reading the paper while I asked the question, slowly looked up from what he was reading, took off his glasses, and looked at me. Before he said anything, Daddy started laughing. Not one of those throaty laughs. No, this laugh started somewhere in his gut. It had lain dormant until this moment when my request was made. As the laughter built, I could hear my father saying as I left the room, "What you need an allowance for? You live free, you eat free, and shoot, you think about it, you should be paying me."

Anthony Webb

Well, after that brief verbal exchange, the subject of an allowance was never discussed between the two of us again. But mysteriously, when I turned thirteen, my lunch money doubled from a dollar fifty to three dollars without any explanation.

Two days before my fifteenth birthday, an event occurred that would change my life as I knew it: my youngest brother was born. His birth came just forty-eight hours before my birthday, which for most households would be a time of celebration. Willie and Daniel were lukewarm to the announcement, especially since they wanted a sister. I, on the other hand, was furious. The idea of competing with someone else for my mother's attention was downright disturbing to me. With my new brother being born two days before my birthday, I was really pissed off. All of the attention that I was supposed to receive for my birthday was lost to the celebration of my new brother's birth, which sucked.

Two months after the arrival of Rob Jr., my parents made a decision that further intensified my disregard for the newest member of the family. One day in the fall, I came home after a grueling day at school. I passed Willie and Daniel as they headed toward their bedrooms. Daniel stopped me and said, "Mama wants you, but just remember we had nothing to do with it."

"With what?" I asked.

"Ask Mama. She will tell you. But remember we had nothing to do with it—nothing."

Daniel ran to his room. I shook my head and went looking for my mother.

I walked into the living room, and there sat my mother, engaged in her daily routine of watching the afternoon soap operas before my dad got home from work. I greeted her, but before I could ask her about Daniel's comments, she said, "Jamie, me and your father have been talking and we decided to moved Willie and Daniel into your bedroom. So since you are the oldest, you need to help your brothers bring their beds into your bedroom."

I looked at her, smiling meekly, and said, "Yes, ma'am."

So that evening, I helped move a set of bunk beds, a dresser, and two of my brothers into my room, while the baby, Rob Jr., slept restfully in what was now his private room.

In all honesty, the events that happened next were not all my brothers' faults, although they did play a major part. Two weeks after the big move, my beloved goldfish Alicia was found mysteriously floating at the top of the aquarium. Willie was the first to acknowledge Alicia in her lifeless state. He came into the kitchen as I was finishing up my breakfast and said, "Jamie, something happened to Alicia."

"Something like what?"
"I don't know. She doesn't look well."

As I ran up the steps, I dreaded the worst, and her stiff body floating upside down confirmed my fears. I stood in front of the fish bowl, shaking, unable to say a word.

Daniel, who was in the bathroom, came out, reviewed the situation, and did what every child would have done in that situation. He started to holler, "Mama, Mama, come quick. Jamie is acting crazy."

Well, my mother, bless her heart, does not have a quick bone in her body, but she came as fast as she could. But instead of Mama coming to me to soothe my sorrow, she yelled up the stairs, "You boys stop making so much noise; you'll wake the baby."

"But Mama," said Daniel, "Jamie's still shaking."
"Jamie, you stop all that shaking and come back down stairs and finish your breakfast. It's too early for all this foolishness, because if that baby wakes up, you will be doing more than shaking. You hear me, Jamie? I'm talking to you."

There you have it: my emotional reaction to the death of my beloved goldfish described as foolishness. And on top of that, my mother demanded acknowledgment that I heard and will obey her edict. Always seeking to please my mother, so as to be viewed as the good son, I said, "Yes, ma'am," and pretended to suppress my feelings. But before I returned downstairs, I looked both my brothers in the eye and said under my breath so that my mother could not hear me, "This is not over and someone will pay for this."

While finishing my breakfast, I explained to my mother that I suspected foul play was the cause of Alicia's death. She laughed.

"But Ma, when I left the bedroom, she was still alive."

With laughter still in her voice, my mother tried to explain to me the way of the world, that things happen. But then a serious look overcame her. She looked out somewhere in my direction, but beyond me, and said, "Jamie, when the death angel is ready, he's ready, and nothing and no one can stop him from completing his duty. It was just Alicia's time."

She stared off into space for a while. Maybe in thinking about Alicia's death, my mama uncovered some unresolved sorrow from past situations. I do not know. But I did see her wipe her eyes. I was still dejected by her explanation. I was seeking sympathy and only got common-sense poppycock.

"Yes, ma'am."

I don't know if she even knew that I had left; she was still in the same spot with the same look when I went back upstairs. Knowing now that I would not get any support from my mother—and I was not foolish enough to involve my father—I set out on my own to determine Alicia's cause of death.

My initial investigation was fruitless; both of the prime suspects were non-cooperative. A break in the case occurred when later that day Daniel became upset at Willie about something and disclosed that Willie had been secretly adding salt to Alicia's water every day. Apparently, Willie was learning about saltwater fish in science class. He had asked Daniel if Alicia was a saltwater goldfish. Daniel told

Willie that he did not think so. But Willie wanted to know for himself, so he set up this little experiment of adding a little salt each day to Alicia's water after I had gotten up and gone into the bathroom.

This morning, while putting the salt in the fish bowl, Willie stumbled and more salt was dumped in than planned. Although Willie tried to get the excess salt out of the bowl, it was too late. Daniel, who saw the whole thing from the top bunk bed, ran into the bathroom and shut the door. The next thing Daniel heard was Willie in the kitchen talking about something being wrong with Alicia. To calm Daniel's fears of retaliation from Willie, I promised that I would not reveal him as the source of my information. I knew that what Daniel confessed to me was the truth; I also knew that if I presented this evidence to my parents, nothing would be done, so I just waited.

Since I was still seething from Alicia's death, my brothers attempted to stay clear of me. They did not initiate interaction, nor did I. The only time we were in the same space was when we ate and slept. Because I had lost my sanctuary, I started spending more time outside of the house, which suited everyone, especially my brothers.

On the first Saturday of my summer vacation, I noticed that Dad and Mr. Joe, his best friend, were bringing wood paneling into the house and taking it up to the third floor. At this time, "the third floor," as we called it, was an unfinished, cold, spooky, and dusty space. By the end of the weekend, rumor had it that the floor had been changed into a two-bedroom living space. I was truly afraid to ask my mother whom the bedrooms were for. Maybe they were planning to adopt two more children, or maybe Aunt May from down south was coming to live with us. Our mother told us not to go up to the third floor because Daddy was not finished working up there.

I did not sleep a wink the next night as I tried to figure why my parents had those bedrooms built. With the suspense urging me on, I slipped out of bed and quietly made my way up the steps to the third floor before anyone had awakened. I immediately noticed that the old musty smell had been replaced with a clean, new scent. I turned on the light to gaze upon my father's handiwork. The rooms made the attic seem bigger and brighter. But before I could truly inspect the rooms, I heard the unmistakable sound of someone coming up the creaky third-floor steps.

I was doomed, and since there was no place to hide, I just stood there, hoping the person, or spirit, would not see me. Stupid idea, because it was my dad. I nearly shit my pants. He walked past me, not even glancing in my direction, and inspected the walls. Dad just stood there staring at the wall, and then he slowly turned in my direction and said, "Very good work, would you say so?"

Scared as heck, I answered, "Yes, sir. Very good work."

Dad looked me in the eye and said, "You know, Jamie, I'm proud of the way you handled the situation with your brothers; I know it was not fair. But as you will learn, life is not always fair. Your mother and I decided it was only right for you to have your room back, so we had these two rooms built for your brothers. You are my oldest son, and I look to you to set the way for your younger brothers."

He shook my hand and disappeared down the steps. I stood there, stunned, unable to comprehend the moment. My restrained father had told me that he was proud of me, his oldest son, and I, Jamie Turner, should set the way for my brothers. Wow! I was floored.

I stood there for a long time, thinking about my father's words before going back downstairs. Not surprisingly, the conversation was never mentioned again, and my father continued to treat me indifferently. But now I knew in my heart of hearts how my father felt about me, and that was enough for me.

CHAPTER 7

Garden Time

"Well, let's get this show on the road."
"I haven't had breakfast yet."
"That's too bad."

Laughter fills the porch; the war of words has begun between the brothers, with the first victim being Jamie—the unofficial mama's boy of the family. Jamie's closeness to his mother has always been a sore spot for his brothers. Behind his back, his brothers would call him the "golden child," a name given to one who thinks they are better than others. Trying to get as much attention off of himself as possible, Jamie smiles and says, "You guys are just jealous that I have two women who love me so much and you suckers have none."

Looking toward Willie for a quick escape, Jamie then says, "So mayor, you're mighty quiet. What's happening?"

The "mayor," as Willie is unofficially known as in the neighborhood, is the title that the brothers gave to him long ago. He was bestowed with this title because in their neighborhood, there is not one person who lives there, nor one event that occurs, that Willie does not know about. Except for his brief marriage and his short-lived college career, Willie has always lived the Turner house, which is located in an area of the city called Glenville. Once the home of a large Jewish population in the early fifties, Glenville now is one hundred percent African American—and Willie is its unofficial mayor.

Clearing his throat like he is about to sing, Willie cocks his head to the side and rubs his chin. The brothers brace themselves, because they know that Willie is preparing to do what he does best—that is, gossip. Not known to be a hard worker, Willie could gossip and stir up more mess than anyone in the neighborhood.

"Well," he starts, "Things are quiet around here since those thieving Gardner boys got locked up. There is a new family moving in around the street and they look like trouble—"

But before Willie can finished his review of the happenings in the neighborhood, Mrs. Turner interrupts him by saying, "Boy, I do not care how much you rub your chin. If you lazy bums do not get your asses off this porch and into that garden, you are going to be the news of the neighborhood."

With those well-expressed sentiments, the brothers quickly consider their options and, with the exception of Rob Jr., head toward the garden.

As his brothers gather the garden supplies and tools to take to the garden, Rob Jr. sits on the porch, watching and thinking. He has always detested this time of year when they have to work in the garden. There was something about getting all sweaty, dirty, and funky that did not sit well with Rob Jr. When he was a child and this time of year approached, Rob Jr. would plead to his mother to do some other chore besides working in the garden. Sometimes it would work, but generally it did not. When he was a teenager, his parents finally allowed him to exchange his garden service for housework. Although Rob Jr.'s pleading did eventually get him out of the garden, cleaning the house was no cushy job. Along with the verbal abuse that he received from his brothers for not helping in the garden, the Turners' house was a good size. There were two bathrooms, four bedrooms, a basement, a sitting room, a living room, a kitchen, wall-to-wall carpet, stairs, and numerous nooks and crannies that needed vacuuming, scrubbing, and dusting.

For some reason today, Rob Jr. did not move when his brothers began gathering their garden tools. At that time, he would typically begin to locate his cleaning products, but not today. Rob Jr. wanted to be with his brothers, so instead of going into the house, as he usually did, he head down the steps toward the garden. Mrs. Turner looks and yells to Rob Jr., "Where you going?"

"Well, I haven't seen Daniel in a couple of months and I want to talk something over with him. Anyway, I think it's time for me to find out why these guys like working in the garden so much. Who knows? I may be back sooner than you think."

"Good boy," says Mrs. Turner as she laughs.

She smiles as she watches her youngest son cross the street to join his brothers. "Yes, yes," she says softly. "That's where you belong, alongside your brothers in the garden. Thank you, Jesus."

As Rob Jr. walks across the street, thoughts of doom enter his psyche. Although he did desire to talk to somebody about what was going on, why did he choose this moment to reveal himself to his brothers, especially that overanalytical Daniel? Anxiety forms in Rob Jr.'s mind as he continues to second-guess his decision, making him pay less attention on where he is going. While attempting to open the garden gate, Rob Jr. trips over his feet. As he stumbles through the gate trying to catch himself, his brothers burst out laughing.

Willie shouts out, "Haven't you learned how to walk yet, boy? And what are doing out here anyway? What does your mother want with us now?"

Trying to act like that did not just happen, Rob Jr. picks up a garden hoe that is leaning against the fence, examines the blade, and looks directly at Willie, who is still laughing. "Why all the questions, Willie? You taking your job as mayor a little too far. You the man now?" He said this without cracking a smile.

"First of all, I do not know if Mama wants you or not. But anyway, this time I'm not the messenger. I've come to help you bums in the garden."

Rob Jr. places the garden hoe squarely in front of him, waiting nervously to hear his brother's response. Their laughter has stopped and has been replaced with silence.

After what seems like a billion years to Rob Jr., Jamie yells, "Well, I'll be damned. It's about time. We have been waiting a long time for this moment. So you want to work in the garden with your big brothers. Come over here and let me give you a big hug."

Laughter erupts again among the group as they embrace their youngest brother, welcoming him into the final phase of his rites of passage—working in the garden. But before Jamie can take Rob Jr. off to the side to tell him about the true history of the garden, Willie says, "Hey, just before you start with your speech making, mama's boy, let the boy get some work done first."

"Who are you calling mama's boy, mayor?" replies Jamie. "I'm just going to give my little brother some pointers about working in the garden, but never mind. You guys are just a pain in the butt, especially you Willie. Where is my garden hoe?"

Jamie shakes his head as he goes in search of his garden tool. He is disappointed that that simple Willie cut his time with Rob Jr. short. Jamie wanted to get to Rob Jr. before Daniel did; he needed Rob Jr. on his side.

Rob Jr. looks around the garden, attempting to figure out what each brothers does in the garden. Daniel is pulling some small green plants out of white containers near the fence with a look of contentment on his face. *Those darn plants must be made out of gold,* thinks Rob Jr. as he watches his older brother gently brush the leaves of several plants.

As long as Rob Jr. can remember, Daniel had always been the one who enjoyed being different. The family had always secretly questioned whether Daniel was comfortable in his blackness since he enjoyed doing non-black things like going camping, listening to classical music, and occasionally dating outside of his race. That last item did not sit well with his mother, as Rob Jr. fondly recalls, but Daniel was his favorite brother, the one whose courage he admired. From the corner of his eye, Rob Jr. sees that Jamie has moved to the other corner of the garden, isolating himself from everyone. Out of a bag, he pulls something that looks like dried-out pieces of potatoes.

Rob Jr. realizes that he barely knows his oldest brother. The ten-year gap in age has been a difficult barrier to cross. Rob Jr. and Jamie had not shared a lot of time together growing up. Jamie was in college and then moved away while Rob Jr. was going through his initial growing pains; therefore, they never meshed like he and Daniel had. Rob Jr. had even heard that Jamie was jealous of him for being the baby of the family because of all the attention he received from his mother. But Rob Jr. never paid any attention to that type of talk. He just thought that his oldest brother was special.

Since Daniel was in his own world, and Jamie was on the other side of the garden, Rob Jr. sought out Willie, who was leaning against the fence, doing nothing, as usual. Rob Jr. had little patience with his brother who was closest to him in age. Willie and Rob Jr.'s relationship had always been tentative, depending on what either one needed from the other. Rob Jr. thought that Willie never treated him like a brother, while Willie viewed him as a spoiled brat.

"So what do you guys need help with?" Rob Jr. asked Willie.

"Hey, I'm a farmhand like you. You better asked Daniel. He is the head nigger in charge out here."

"Why do you always have to use the *n* word?"

"What? You mean nigger?"

"Yea, that word. Is it a word of endearment for you? Or have you yet to evolve into the twenty-first century?"

"What are you talking about, nigger?"

"You know, Jamie is right. You are an asshole."

Willie just smiles and shakes his head, saying, "Jamie said that about me. I'll be … You two niggers are too easy. Just too easy."

Rob Jr. walks away with his head shaking also, but for a different reason. He approaches Daniel who is watering cabbage plants in the corner of the garden.

"So what's with Willie?"
"What do you mean?"
"Never mind. I was told that you are in charge of this motley crew. What do you want me to do?"

Daniel looks up for the first time at his youngest brother. Rob Jr. was not as tall as him and had a slimmer build. He had what was called a "pretty boy" look—always well dressed, neat, and smelling good. Along with being well educated, Rob Jr. was the toast of the family. In a way, Daniel admired his younger brother; he was everything that he was not. It was his contention that with Rob Jr., his parents finally got it right.

"Well, let's see. Hmm, you take those tomato plants over there next to the wheelbarrow and plant them in that third row next to the fence, and make sure you tie them up with stakes. I will show you how to do it right."

Rob Jr. watches Daniel gently remove an individual tomato plant from its container. After placing the tomato plant in predug hole, Daniel carefully fills the hole with fertilizer and soil. Daniel examines the wooden stakes that Willie had brought over and, after much deliberation, chooses one. He places the stake close to the tomato plant and secures the two together with string. From the look on Daniel's face, you would have thought that he had found the cure for cancer.

After a hands-on demonstration from Daniel, Rob Jr. is convinced that he had what to do down pat. After doing two plants under Daniel's watchful eye, Rob Jr. is reassured that he has it all together.

For some reason, Rob Jr. feels good receiving praise from Daniel for his transplanting work. Rob Jr. looks up toward Daniel and says, "I can remember as a little boy that you guys always seemed to be working in the garden all summer long, so I said to myself then that I would never work in that garden. No, not me."

"So that's why you always cried when Mama told you to work in the garden?"

"Yep, I didn't want to spend my whole summer digging holes and picking beans. I just thought that this was exhausting work and working in the house would be easier. Boy, I was wrong. I think Mama purposely made the house dirtier on the day I was supposed to clean it. I came to really hate Memorial Day weekend."

"So what made you come out here with us today?"

"Well, I thought it was just time. By the way, how long have you been working in the garden?"

"We just started, asshole," says a laughing Willie, who had brought over more stakes for Rob Jr. to use.

"No, not now, but how old were you when you guys started in the garden?"

"That's a good question, Rob Jr."

While pulling a brown leaf off a cabbage plant, Daniel responds, "I guess I was about nine years old, and you must have been two years old. Yea, I was in the third grade, in Mrs. McGhee's class, when your mother sentenced me to this life as a field nig—*hand*. I brought home a flyer about a garden program sponsored by the school, and next thing I know, Mama had enrolled me in the school garden program. So Ma and I dug up a small patch of ground over there behind the garage, and thus the garden was born from those humble beginnings. The next year, if I remember correctly, Mama enrolled Jamie in the program and we have been out here ever since. Isn't that right, Jamie?"

Jamie looks up from planting white potatoes plants and brushes the dirt from his hands. Although he is on the other side of the garden, he can still hear the conversation between his brothers.

Why in the hell does he always have to remind me that it was him and not me who started the garden? thinks Jamie. *And now he is attempting to belittle me even more by telling Rob Jr. the same line of bull.*

"It's just as Daniel stated. It was Mama and him who started the garden," Jamie replies coldly.

With eyes that could kill, Jamie stares at Daniel and whispers under his breath, "Yes, Daniel, the blessed one."

What Jamie really wanted to tell Rob Jr. earlier, before Willie interrupted him, was that although Daniel was first to have a garden, it was his idea. He can remember talking to Daniel about starting a garden. Jamie believed that it would please his mother since she told him that she grew up in the country. But he was too scared to ask his mother about starting one since he had recently gotten in trouble, so he told Daniel ask her. To Jamie's regret, Mrs. Turner praised Daniel for coming up with such a thoughtful idea. She in turn scolded Jamie when he attempted unsuccessfully to get credit for the idea. With Daniel beaming in his mother's glory, Jamie festered with envy. He viewed his brother's action as an act of unforgiveable treason. Like Jacob and Esau in the Bible, Daniel, the younger brother, received the blessing of his parents that the older son thought he deserved, which has always pissed off Jamie. But instead of telling Rob Jr. his version of the story or how he felt, Jamie turns his attention to his adversary, Daniel. Just thinking about what Daniel had done makes the usually cool and calm Jamie upset. For some reason, that day he has had enough. His false demeanor has been compromised and Jamie is about to show his true self.

Jamie moves toward Daniel, pointing at him, while stating in a slightly irritated voice, "It's all about you, Daniel. It's all about you."

Daniel looks in bewilderment at Jamie, trying to figure out what is the matter with him. With no time to figure out his older brother's behavior, Daniel backs up until he is cornered against the fence. He forces a smile and says, "It must be the sun, Jamie. I think that you are about to blow a fuse."

Just at that moment, Daniel trips over the water hose, somehow triggering the sprinklers, and the brothers scatter in all directions, laughing as they run. The unpredicted shower was successful in relieving the tension of the moment, and the laughter lasted for a while as Willie retold the story over and over. Jamie uses this moment to save face and laugh off his behavior, while all the time hiding his true feelings. All appears to be well with the Turner boys.

From her majestic perch on the porch, Mrs. Turner observes every interaction in the garden, experiencing a feeling that had been missing since the passing of her husband. As she closes her eyes to thank her God for this moment, Mrs. Turner hears her name being called. "Helena, Helena, you asleep?"

It is the woman who has been her next-door neighbor for thirty years, Betty Washington. "Helena, ain't that Daniel out there in the garden? Boy, he sure is skinny. When did he get home? Helena, don't you hear me?"

"I'm not asleep. And yes, that's Daniel, and yes, he is skinny."

"I know he must be glad to be home to get some of your good old cooking."

Trying not to be rude to her nosy neighbor, but keeping her eyes fixed on her boys, Mrs. Turner answers, "Yea, I'm very glad that he is home too."

After untangling from the water hose, Daniel looks across the street and sees his mother still sitting on the porch, talking to someone. *Hmmm,* he thought, *that's Mrs. Betty. I haven't seen her for a while, but it does not appear that she has missed any meals.*

He smiles and waves in her direction and then focuses his attention back to the day's task. Someone's cell phone rings, and suddenly, the world turns for one of the brothers.

CHAPTER 8

Bev

"Robert Turner, why are you in my hallway?" inquired Mrs. Ryan.

That was my introduction to Robert: in a hallway on my first day at Iowa Maple Elementary School. We had just moved to Cleveland from Norfolk, Virginia, and I needed to get registered for school. So my mother took me to the neighborhood school, and there we stood, listening to Mrs. Ryan, the principal, reprimand a skinny black boy who had the cutest eyes, as she walked us to my new classroom.

"Robert Turner, if I have told you once, I have told you twice: no one misbehaves in my school. I do not know the reason why you are standing outside your classroom, but it better be for getting an A on an exam, or you are going to be in big trouble."

All the while Mrs. Ryan is speaking to Robert, he had the "Who me? Not me!" look, and I felt sorry for him. My mother looked at me, saying sternly, "You see that boy over there? That's the one you should stay away from, Beverly."

"Yes, ma'am."

I took a long look, knowing that my future was directly linked to the misguided boy with the cute eyes, though I did not know just how yet. I didn't see Robert again until three days later; the buzz in the classroom was that he had gotten suspended. By the time he returned to school, I had the school routine down pat and was receiving the attention of certain males in the classroom, which caused friction with a couple of my female peers, especially that darned Linda Jones. Unbeknownst to Miss Jones, I did not desire Daniel Malone's or Thomas Doaty's attention. My heart was set on the forbidden fruit named Robert Turner Jr.

Throwing my mother's warning to the wind, I set out to obtain what I felt was rightly mine. Robert, being Robert, was too cool to attempt any boyish prank to win my affection like his male counterparts; he just ignored me, which pissed me off. But soon fate brought together what I could not.

Mr. Tucker, our teacher, paired Robert and me together as study partners, which when announced to the class caused Linda Jones to holler out, "Oh no!"

For effect, I made a face that suggested I was quite upset with the pairing, though inside, my heart was saying, "Yes, yes!"

So convincing was my false face that after school, Mr. Tucker pulled me to the side and said, "Beverly, I know that you are upset with being Robert's study partner, but remember it's only for six weeks, and then we will switch."

"Well, Mr. Tucker, I have given it some thought. I know it was not the pairing I thought I would receive, but my parents have taught me that things in life happen for a reason, so I think that I will work well with Robert."

"Well, Beverly that's quite a grownup way of looking at things. I think that you can be a positive influence on Robert."

"Well, I hope so."

With that, I gave Mr. Tucker a deceptive sigh, waved good-bye, and ran all the way home with a smile on my face. Since the first day I saw Rob Jr. in the hallway being berated by Mrs. Ryan, I knew that he was my soul mate. Yes, I know that the term *soul mate* is a big word for a fourth grader, but I had read an article in my cousin's *Cosmo* magazine that talked about it. So when girls my age were looking for a boy to like, I was searching for my soul mate. I guess my mother was correct when she would constantly tell me "Beverly, you are too big for your britches."

One of the reasons that Rob Jr.'s boyish good looks did not directly affect me was an understanding that I already knew that he was mine. How I knew that, I really could not explain. It was just that it was supposed to be. Even Rob Jr. knew there was something different about me, but he could not figure it out—not initially anyway.

The study partner pairing worked well. Robert soon discovered that math was one of my strengths, and it was quite apparent from his grades that it was his weakness. An unspoken alliance was formed between us. Robert received the assistance that he needed to pass fourth grade math, and I received praise from Mr. Tucker and, most importantly, one-on-one time with Robert. It was a win-win situation for the both of us. I believed that my nonchalant attitude, along with my superior math ability, finally won him over. I could never say that Rob Jr. and I were close; I think what we displayed toward each other was respect. Through the establishment of respect, a bond was created between the two of us. While never verbalized, we knew of its existence. We were never boyfriend and girlfriend. No, that seemed too petty, too possessive for me. So what developed was my first authentic friendship—authentic in that we were able to share feelings, as much as two fourth graders could share them.

The summer after fifth grade, my family moved to South Carolina. When I heard the news that we were moving, I nearly fainted. I remember coming into the kitchen after school, dropping my books on the table, and then walking into the living room. There, sitting on the couch, were my parents and my younger brother, Bruce. Bruce saw me and ran toward me, yelling, "Guess what? We moving again! Granddad is sick, and we're moving down south to take care of him."

"What? Mama, is this true? We're moving down south. Tell me it ain't true."

After my mom scolded me for using the word *ain't* in a sentence, she calmly told me that Bruce was half telling the truth. My dad was being reassigned to a base in South Carolina, which would allow us to help support her father who was recovering from a stroke. Her words became lost in my head as my thoughts drifted to Rob Jr. I had just found my soul mate, and I was already being pulled away from him—how cruel can life be. I stared in disbelief at my mom, unable to say a word, incapable of describing the pain that I felt.

After we moved, I thought that my life was over and God had left me for dead. I believed that I would never see Rob Jr. again. Although we promised to write each other, it never happened. I wrote Rob Jr. five times that summer, but never received a letter back from him. Every day during the summer I would check the mailbox, sometimes twice, and every day I would come back disappointed.

Just before school started, I had lost all hope in my reluctant soul mate and tried to forget him. Surprisingly, it worked; I guess when you have no hope, none can arise. Even at eleven years old, I knew that I had found someone special—not always great, wonderful, or polite, but special. My mom, bless her heart, tried to explain my feelings for Rob Jr. as puppy love. Boy, was she wrong. First of all, I never told my mom that I loved him; I just mentioned that he made me feel good when I was around him. She, with her adult mind, equated feeling good with love, which I did not agree with. Adults can sometimes complicate the simplest things. As I grew older, I would learn that the love that my mom was talking about was not based on reality but rather media-created fantasy. This became even more apparent when my loving parents divorced, and then again when my short-lived first marriage failed. At an early age, I resolved that how a person made you feel when you were around them was more important than if you loved them or not—and Rob Jr. had made me feel good. That feeling didn't come back for a long time, because the next time I saw Rob Jr., it was one failed marriage, two college degrees, and a miscarriage later.

Twenty-three years later, in an attempt to get my life back on track, I prepared to go back to school, an area were I have always been successful. At thirty-four years old with a broken marriage behind me, I felt that I needed to break clean out of the box in which I was now living. Having slaved for five years at a community mental health agency as a psychotherapist, I was burnt out, unsatisfied, and poor. I knew the only way to the big bucks was to obtain the highest degree possible, the elusive PhD. So I began applying to graduate programs in clinical psychology throughout the country.

I was so determined to get out of my carefully planned yet unsuccessful life that I told myself that I would attend the first clinical psychology program that accepted me. To my surprise, the first acceptance letter was from Case Western Reserve University, and as fate had determined, the school was in Cleveland, Ohio. I had long since left Cleveland and its memories behind, stuffed somewhere in a box in some closet. Of all places, fate chose to return me to Cleveland—well, I thought, a plan is a plan. So I packed my bags, said my good-byes, and headed off.

As I drove to my new home, I thought back to the last few weeks. Telling my clients that I was leaving was quite emotional for them and me; even my pain-in-the ass client, Ms. Adrian, seemed to treat me better in those last days. I had a moving sale and sold everything, with the exception of my computer, a book or two, and some clothes. I wanted to start fresh, with few reminders of my past. It is amazing how many people enjoy buying other people's stuff.

Driving toward Cleveland, I thought about Rob Jr., whom I had not spoken to since we were ten years old. He had probably married that sneaky Linda Jones. She was always jealous of our friendship; she could not wait to get to her hands all over him after I left, which probably resulted in five snotty-nosed children. It serves him right; I was his soul mate, not her. Well, I did not really save myself for him, either. My marriage to Johnny was doomed before it even started, and the affair with Carl did not help. Life has a funny way of getting even with you.

I never have believed in love, and I never thought that someone's feelings about me could satisfy me. Nah, I was never that foolish. But looking back, I did not believe in Santa Claus or the Easter bunny either. I guess I have a need to touch, to taste, and to see something to believe it is true. Because my family moved from army base to army base in my youth, my friendships have been fleeting and few. I have always attempted to keep myself in the present and not look beyond tomorrow—a difficult cognitive process for sure. My failed relationships have mainly been due to my refusal to look to the future. My ex desired a stereotypical wife, not one who could think beyond the kitchen and bedroom. I made a moral error in my marriage, a youthful regrettable error. After several unsuccessful attempts to change my ex, I said, "Fuck it," and started to mess around with Carl.

Not surprisingly, my affair with Carl had more potential than my marriage because it was based in the present, with no regrets. But our relationship was another short-lived interaction, due to Carl's inability to stimulate anything beyond my vagina, which became boring to me. Sure, it was a step up from my husband, but a small step. I desired him to stimulate other parts of me, like my mind or even my clit. I really do not believe the asshole even knew what or where my clit was or that I had a mind. Men are just assholes.

My first day at Case was an orientation for the incoming doctoral candidates. There were eight of us, and two of my peers looked like carbon copies of me, but eight years younger and much prettier. During our lunch break, one of the carbon copies introduced herself as Cathy and asked me if I wanted to walk over to the student union for food. Reluctantly, I agreed, and in just one short hour, I learned more about Cathy than anyone would care to know.

She was from Tennessee and the first from her family to attend college. Though her father wanted her to stay at home to become a housewife for one of Tennessee's finest, Cathy had wanted more for her life. So the day after she graduated from high school, Cathy packed her bags and took the Greyhound to Knoxville, the big city. She waited tables while living in a one-bedroom "shithole," as she called it, before enrolling at the University of Tennessee. Cathy graduated with one of those cum laude words behind her name. If she had lived out her father's wishes, she would be just another redneck housewife with a boatload of babies, but today she is a PhD candidate at one of the most prestigious universities in America.

I guess timing, location, and perception are everything. There is something to say about keeping your dreams alive. Needless to say, this was more than I wanted to know about anyone during our first social interaction. But her openness allowed me to not have to disclose anything about myself, which was cool with me. Before there was an opening for me to say anything, we had ordered our lunch and were on the way back to the orientation.

After lunch, the PhD candidates were to meet with their mentor professors, who they would be studying under. I was assigned Dr. Megan Smith, a fifteen-year veteran of the department. She had written several books and journal articles on cross-cultural psychology, an area that I planned to research. Dr. Smith displayed a laid-back persona, which made us a good match. One of the requirements for being a research assistant was to teach an undergraduate psychology class. This was a challenge for me because I had never taught anything in my life.

On the first day of my class, my anxiety was through the roof. I changed my outfit at least five times, trying to look scholarly without appearing like a square. I arrived to my classroom thirty minutes early and there were two students already there. *Oh my,* I thought, *what have I signed up for?* I smiled at them and sat down at my desk to wait for the beginning of class. Thirty-five minutes later, as I stood in front of my abnormal psychology class, he walked back into my life.

I took a big breath and started class at 6:00 p.m. By that time, there were twenty-four students in attendance. After introducing myself and telling the students what my expectations were, most of the nervousness was gone. *This is not much different from running group therapy,* I thought.

Five minutes later, while I was writing some information on the board, the door opened and he walked in the room. He cautiously approached me at the board, speaking in a hushed voice, "Excuse me, my name is Robert Turner Jr. I'm sorry that I'm late, but I do not understand why my name was not on the class list located on the wall outside of class. I have my registration right here in my hand."

Not knowing what to say, I went to my desk to review my attendance sheet. As he stood there waiting for answer, I studied him quickly. *Yep, that's him,* I thought. Although I was smiling on the inside, my facial expression did not change. I stated in my most professional voice, "What class are you looking for, Mr. Turner? You did say Robert Turner?"

He unfolded his schedule and read, "Yes, Robert Turner Jr. Mmm, social psychology 476."

"'Well," I said, "that is why your name does not appear on the attendance sheet; that class is being taught by Dr. Jones across the hall in 36B."

A look of embarrassment appeared on his face as he quickly said, "I'm sorry. Thanks," and ran to his classroom. As I tried to transition back to what I was doing prior to his arrival, I smiled, and that smile did not leave my face during the whole lecture. Focusing back to the task at hand, I was able to finish class with time to spare. I excused my students ten minutes early with a stern warning that this would be the last time we would be leaving so early. After the class left, I erased the board, collected my things, and waited outside the room to reintroduce myself to my soul mate.

CHAPTER 9

Warriors' Breakfast

"Whose phone is that?" asked Willie. "Is that yours, Rob Jr.?"

Indeed, it was Rob Jr.'s phone. He jumped to look to see who was calling. When Bev's name appeared on the phone, his heart beat a little quicker.

Why now? thought Rob Jr. It was the call that he wanted, but not the place where he wanted to receive it. Regrettably, he answered, with all of his brothers' eyes on him. They heard him say, "Hi, sweetie."

"Well, yes, I'm over at my mother's house digging up the garden with my brothers."

"Yep."

"What's that? What?"

"Oh."

"Oh."

"Okay."

"Okay, I will call you when I'm finished."

"It will be fine."

"Bye, baby. Love you."

"Well, that was short and sweet," said Willie.

"Mind your own business, Willie," answered Rob Jr.

Although the conversation lasted less than a minute, the information exchanged was life changing for Rob Jr. Generally, Rob Jr. would be concerned about what his brothers thought about him. Being worried about what other people thought of him has always been one of Rob Jr.'s stumbling blocks. But not this time. Now he needed to think and get away from that smart ass Willie.

As Willie continued to mock Rob Jr., Daniel resumed digging holes for the tomato plants, pretending not to pay attention to the goings-on. *My, my,* thought Daniel. *It appears that the young Rob Jr. is in love.* A disabled veteran of the romantic wars, Daniel observed the telltale look of stupor that appeared on Rob Jr.'s face after the phone call and incorrectly assumed love was the cause. Daniel differed from Willie in his approach, however. Willie saw it as a news item, while Daniel made a mental note to mention it at a later date.

It was about 10:30 a.m. With the surprise addition of Rob Jr., Daniel calculated that all the planting, watering, and touch-ups should be completed by early afternoon. He reached down to clump the soil in his fist, which had been recently tilled by the city. Daniel rolled it slowly in his hand while bringing it up to his nose to smell. He closed his eyes. It felt damp in his hands and gave off a musky earth scent.

Daniel looked content, knowing his bond with the earth continues. Like his mother and his great aunt May before her, Daniel had a true connection with nature. It is possible this was one of the few traits he shares with his mother. Daniel knew that he was not the favorite son, and because of his less-than status, clashes with his mother were common. He remembered the time he told his mother about Barbara, one of his early girlfriends. You would have thought World War III had occurred. Daniel had purposefully left out the fact that Barbara was white until his mother had agreed to have her over for dinner. It was not until Jamie revealed Barbara's racial heritage to his mother two days before Thanksgiving dinner that all hell exploded. Mrs. Turner called Daniel every name in the book, indicating in very descriptive terms her disappointment in him. The verbal assault continued for over an hour, with Daniel taking his beating without responding, which infuriated his mother even more. Unknown to his mother and Jamie was that Barbara never was coming to dinner—because Daniel had not invited her. He was smart enough to predict his mother's reaction to one of her sons dating someone outside their racial group; however, he was surprised by his big brother's betrayal. Although Daniel never approached Jamie directly about the incident, he quietly recorded it in his mental file.

Daniel brought over a basket filled with seeds, along with an assortment of tomatoes, peppers, cabbages, and collard plants—the results of their mother's seed catalog purchases over the winter. The seeds in the baskets were carefully placed in the order their mother wanted them planted. First the carrots, then the okra, and then the beans. Always the same order, year after year. Daniel shook his head and thought, *Those damn carrots again. I've told her a million times that it's cheaper to buy them in the store than to grow them, but does she listen?*

"Jamie!" yells Daniel.

Jamie had just begun to mark off the garden by placing wooden stakes in the intended rows. He reluctantly turned in Daniel's direction upon hearing his name called, wondering what Judas wanted now. Jamie knew that he had to play cool because he had lost it earlier. He took a couple of deep breaths and counted to ten before answering his brother.

It had always been Jamie's belief that since he was the oldest, he should be in charge of the garden, not Daniel. That belief had caused Jamie to develop ill feelings toward Daniel. Every year, Jamie internally questioned his participation in this annual ritual. Although Jamie states publicly that he enjoys gardening, his main motive was to force Daniel to share the rewards of the garden with him and his brothers. The rewards, as Jamie sees them, have nothing to do with planting or gathering damn vegetables in the fall but instead are directly related to receiving the love, attention, and admiration that their mother showers on them for their work in the garden. The garden is Mrs. Turner's pride and joy, and those who work in the garden are awarded her blessings. The only reason Jamie allowed himself to be subjected to his younger brother's directives was because he desired his mother's love more than anything else. Unfortunately, Rob Jr.'s presence in the garden meant Jamie's share of his mother's admiration had been even further deceased, and the thought of that made him unhappy.

"Yes, Judas … I mean Daniel."

"Judas? What is that all about? You okay? Anyway, why does your mother continue to tell us to plant carrots when it's cheaper to buy them in the grocery store?"

"You have to ask her, master. I mean Daniel."

"I have. She gives me that look of hers and shakes her head."

"That means shut up and do what I say, master."

After showing Rob Jr. where to plant the tomatoes, Willie took a self-imposed break from working in the garden. He picked up a bottle of water and a folded lawn chair and put himself and the chair under the mulberry tree. Willie took a long gulp of water while glancing over to where his two older brothers were engaged in their never-ending unconscious debate of which one Mama liked best. Willie shook his head. *Assholes,* he thought. *If you guys only knew the truth. You do not have to be a psychologist to deem you two fools stupid and stupider.*

Although living with Mama can be difficult at times, Willie had an opportunity to learn a lot about her. He knew that Rob Jr., the spoiled brat, was his mother's favorite, not those two old fools. As his brothers continued their discussion, a recurring thought resounded in Willie's mind. *What really makes these fools my brothers?* Since he was a child, Willie had always been aware that he was different from his siblings.

Shoot, he thought, *the Cosbys we are not; we do not do things together or even get along that well.*

Not sharing physical features or interests with his brothers made Willie question whether he had a different set of parents. Although he has examined his birth certificate several times, Willie still doubted his place in the family. In his mind, it takes more than a shared bloodline to make individuals brothers, but to his regret he could not put his finger on the source of their differences. Although not the deepest thinker of the family, Willie gave this issue plenty of thought. Using his gift of gab, Willie asked everyone he knew about what it meant to be brothers. From the knowledge gleaned from his informal surveys of friends, Willie concluded that brotherhood is developed through shared experiences among individuals that have the ability to produce some type of emotional connection. Willie felt like that definition still fit his situation: he felt closer to his friends yet desired that same closeness with his brothers.

With his friends, Willie always felt understood, most times without having to say much. He felt the opposite with his brothers; Willie wanted to receive their validation on what he did, instead of their looks of doubts. The question of brotherhood had bothered Willie so much that he actually went to the library to research it. But his efforts were short-lived—not due to a lack of information but because of Willie's insecurities. Like Rob Jr., Willie was always concerned about what others thought of him. Being seen in a library, which is not on his mail route, what would his friends think? Since he was taught by his father not to explain his behavior to others, he decided to put an end to the library research.

Mr. Turner told his boys during one of their exclusive all-male fifth Sunday breakfasts that people will never understand your actions; therefore, you should not try to explain them. Willie smiled recalling those Sunday breakfasts with his father. Whenever a month had a fifth Sunday, the Turner men above the age of twelve had breakfast together, without their mother. Their father's exclusion of the younger Turner males was for two reasons. The officially stated reason was Mr. Turner did not believe that the topics discussed were appropriate for someone younger than twelve. But the main reason, which was never mentioned by their father, was that it allowed their mother to have some company so that she would not sabotage the breakfast. These fifth Sunday father and son meals came to be known as the Breakfast of Warriors. The Breakfast of Warriors was always held at The Good & Tasty diner, a little hole-in-the-wall on Euclid Avenue in East Cleveland. This was the only Sunday that the boys were excused from church, which pleased them to no end.

Mr. Turner had created the Breakfast of Warriors as a means to spend more time with his boys outside of the watchful eye of his wife. While he never openly disagreed with his wife's parenting practices, Mr. Turner did feel that she could be overly protective at times. While Mr. Turner worried that the boys would never develop into men, Mrs. Turner feared that they would not live long enough to become men. Their opposing concerns caused the boys' parents to instill different values in their sons. Mrs. Turner believed that developing a respect for authority was important for the boys; therefore, she had a direct "in your face" approach. Mr. Turner wanted the boys to be able to think on their feet; hence, his indirect storytelling focused on acquiring problem-solving skills.

If you asked Willie what he enjoyed most about those breakfasts, besides the initial exclusion of Rob Jr. because of his age, it would be the stories his father told. He started to think about those stories, but unfortunately for Willie, his time in dreamland was cut short by the watchful eye of his oldest brother.

"Willie, what the heck are you smiling at? Have you lost your mind!" yells Jamie. "Did you hear me asking you to bring over the rest of the fertilizer? Boy, you sure are a lazy ass."

Unmoved by his brother's taunting, Willie looked in his direction and said, "Hey, I was just thinking about those breakfast talks we used to have with Dad. There are times when I wish he were here so I can just listen to him tell those stories. Don't you miss him?"

Jamie's grinning face turns solemn as he feels like he has just been sucker-punched in the stomach. He felt ambushed by Willie. The question touched a nerve deep in his soul, the type of nerve that has the ability to make a person become emotional at any second. This is the part of Jamie's psyche that he kept hidden from everyone but his wife. His brothers did not know that their father's death was quite painful for him. Although he was the oldest, Jamie never liked the idea that he always had to set the example. With his father's passing, Jamie was top dog, a role that he was ill prepared to fill. While Jamie's relationship with his father was strange, he knew that his father loved him unconditionally—unlike his mother's love, which he felt was conditional. Jamie knew that all he had wanted to do since the funeral was to cry and tell his brothers how much he missed their father. But Jamie was the oldest Turner man. He had to set an example of how a Turner man dealt with the ups and downs of life. So today, to prevent himself from becoming too emotional, Jamie looked away from Willie while saying as calmly as he could, "Breakfast meetings with Dad, I remember them. That was a long time ago. I never really enjoyed them, but what does that have to do with the garden?"

The words felt sour as they came out of his mouth. As Jamie turned around to face Willie, he also met the eyes of his other two brothers.

CHAPTER 10

Rob Jr.

Hmm ...

I do believe my oldest brother is facing a dilemma. Why do I think that? Well, because he is standing over there with that "Oh shit, why did I say that?" look on his face—a true sign of a dilemma—as much as I want to make fun of my older brother, I stay silent, knowing that I am facing an even bigger dilemma than Jamie is. I see life's challenges as a series of dilemmas that God has placed before us. I believe your life legacy is determined by the manner in which you overcome your dilemmas. So let me explain my dilemmas.

Bev is pregnant. She found out this morning. Thus the call. Our conversation was short and to the point. I know that I need to go to her, to reassure her, to calm her, but my temporary familial duty requires my presence, which will give me time to think before I see her. I can remember when I first met Bev; we were in the fifth grade. She was a skinny, glasses-wearing, talkative thing, always wanting to prove herself to me. For some reason, I think it was because of her math skills, we became friends. You see, being friends with a female at that age was quite unusual, and for me, being who I was, it was not the coolest thing to do. I believed that Bev, like a lot of girls in that classroom, had a crush on me, but she expressed it differently. Bev was so confident around me that I think I began to have a crush on her. Our friendship emerged clumsily, with all the innocence that two kids bring to it. Then one summer, she left, not to be heard from again for over twenty years.

Fast-forward to last September, my first day of night classes. I had been accepted into the Case Western Reserve University clinical psychology program. Nervous and running late, I accidentally walked into the wrong classroom. When I asked the instructor where the right class was, I heard a voice that I thought I recognized. But due to the tense situation, my brain could not process memory information, so I ignored the feeling.

After one and a half hours of writing notes about Freud and Adler, I left my correct classroom mentally exhausted, having doubts about my return back to college.

In my stupor, I heard the voice again. This time, it pierced my consciousness. I do not know what the voice said, but something inside of me made me holler out, "Bev!" There stood the same instructor whose class I had incorrectly entered with a big smile on her face, saying, "Yep, it's me."

I wore the silliest smile as I looked at a woman who I had not seen since she was a little girl, who I must say time had treated well because she looked wonderful. For a moment, I was speechless. She placed her finger over her mouth to be quiet and then motioned to meet her in five minutes outside the building. Once we were outside in the parking long, Bev told me that since that she was unsure of the policy on teacher-student relationships, she wanted to be a little discreet. But right after she made that statement, she warmly embraced me while laughing. She said, "Got you. I have waited twenty-two years for this moment, and I going to get my hug."

"It's been that long?"
"Yes, too long."

There we stood, just holding each other, with not a word being spoken, in the parking lot like two long-lost lovers who finally found each other. After smiling, hugging, and more smiling, we left each other. Due to the lateness of the hour, we exchanged numbers and made plans to see each other that weekend. As I walked Bev to her car, I was surprised about my emotions toward her. My cool, calm, Turner man demeanor had deserted me, leaving me vulnerable.

Bev even noticed it. She said, "Wow, you have grown up a lot."

"What you mean?"
"Well, the young Rob Jr. would have been cold, stiff, and distant."
"Hmm, well, I'm a big boy now."
"I can see, and I like it."

With those words, Bev jumped in her car, blew me a kiss, and drove away, but not before she reminded me to call her tomorrow about the weekend. *There she goes again,* I thought, *attempting to tell me about myself, just like when we were in fifth grade. I guess some things never change.*

Our outing on Saturday afternoon continued far into the night, and before I knew it, we were a couple. I do not know how she did it, but one day we were long-lost friends and the next day a starry-eyed duo.

Most males would find dating an intelligent, attractive woman a positive situation, but not me. Being romantically involved with Bev has its own set of dilemmas, and that is what I wanted to talk to Daniel about, before this latest one occurred. You see, Bev is white, which could be seen as a dilemma itself by some people. A few unenlightened people, like my mother, have a tendency to hold color against a person, especially females who are in love with their sons. I know that Daniel has dealt with this issue with Mama, so that is why I need to talk to him. I remember a big argument that he had with Mama over one of his girlfriends, who happened to been white. Mama accused him of tricking her into inviting the girl over for Thanksgiving dinner. In his defense, Daniel made one simple statement. "Mama, if she makes me happy, then that is all that should matter, and she does."

Not waiting for a response, Daniel excused himself from the table, packed his bags, said good-bye, and left, and he has yet to return for a Thanksgiving dinner. Surprisingly, nothing was said at that Thanksgiving, or future Thanksgivings, about Daniel's absence or the incident, which I think is amazing. I believe Mama realized that she had overstepped her maternal authority, and to save face, she denies that Daniel exists on Thanksgiving Day. But I am not Daniel, and I enjoy Thanksgiving dinner at the house. I have rarely introduced any of my love interests to my mother, but that streak may be ending soon. With that dilemma looming in the future, the are others gaining strength moment by moment.

I have yet to formulate what I am going to say to Bev, which is yet another dilemma. This is not really new territory for me. Deb, my high school sweetheart, became pregnant when we were seventeen, but she had an abortion before I knew anything about the pregnancy. The incident left me hurt, raw, and confused. I felt betrayed, yet relieved. Betrayed, because I was not involved in the decision, and relieved, for the same reason. The thought of bringing a baby into the world with Deb was scary since we were only kids ourselves, but the idea that we created a living being seemed really cool, thus the confusion. I think that I will play it by ear, console Bev, and listen to what she has to say. Surprisingly, I really do not believe I have a say in the matter, since the baby resides inside of her. Yes, I can attempt to influence her, but in the end, it is her decision. My position will be to support any choice she makes and to reassure her that everything will be all right. I hope it works.

So let me go back and explain why my oldest brother Jamie has a dilemma. Being the youngest child has taught me many things, and one of those lessons was to never speak disrespectfully of the dead. My crazy aunt May schooled me early on in that lesson. We were down south visiting her one summer when I was about eight or nine. Unlike Daniel, who enjoyed visiting our kinfolks, I could have done without knowing that side of the family. Besides my relative's weirdness, it was always so hot, and they had mosquitoes as big as your fist and still no indoor plumbing. Going down south was no treat to me. Then there was my aunt May. She always seemed so different to me, to the point that deep down inside I was scared of her. Wearing those feathers in her hair, making those occasional grunting sounds, and her peculiar style of dressing, my aunt was a strange sight to behold. One night, when the moon was full, I found her rocking and mumbling up a storm under that mulberry tree in back of the house where Mama was born. Being young, stupid, and dumb, I wanted to find out why Aunt May was acting stranger than usual. So I quietly snuck up behind her, making sure I did not step on any dry twigs. Suddenly, in a voice that only the Devil could imitate, I heard, "Boy, don't you know better than to disrespect the dead?"

At that moment, I did not really appreciate what was being said because my feet did not allow my mind to comprehend the message. I ran so fast that I nearly caught up with my shadow. I flew into the bedroom that I was sharing with Daniel, jumped into the bed with my clothes on, and pulled the covers over my head. Daniel later said that sweat was pouring down my face like a faucet when I ran into the room. It was not until my heart stopped racing that I emerged from under the covers and told Daniel what happened.

Like the big brother he was, Daniel calmed me down and explained what Aunt May was doing under the mulberry tree. Although I heard every word Daniel said, there was no amount of reassuring that he could do to make me think that Aunt May was not crazy. He told me that our aunt had a talent, not unlike that of an artist or a singer. She was talking to spirits, which according to Daniel, she was very good at doing. My brother, in his wisdom, attempted to impress on me a different way of looking at people. He stated not to be wary of someone because they are different, since we are more alike than different. It took me many years to understand what the hell he was talking about, but after meeting Bev, it was a lesson that I am glad I was taught. I believe that Jamie is in a lot of trouble with Daddy's spirit because of what he said, thus, his dilemma. *Better him than me*, I thought.

Since I had yet to come to grip with my father's death, I did not need any spirits messing with me. Although it was two years ago, Dad's death still has a hold on me. The whole experience was crazy— or maybe my expectations were out of line. First, support from my friends after the death of my father was nonexistent. My best friend Que Dog, for example, developed the sensitivity of a mule. When my father died, Que Dog became a mute. A guy who could talk a mile a minute when a woman was around suddenly was without words when I most needed him. He later said that he did not know what to say, so he thought it was better to say nothing. The asshole did not know, nor did I tell him, that his silence bothered me more than my well-wishing church members' overly expressive comments. It was like I was Job and he was one of the friends who knew Job was hurting but said nothing.

It is amazing how someone's sorrows can affect the behaviors of people close to him or her. Then there were my church members who made those cute, noncommittal comments like "It's going to be better bye and bye" or "Be thankful he is in a better place." These people almost drove me to drink. *Idiots!* I would mentally yell to them. *My grief has nothing to do with where my father's final resting place is; he's going to a better place. He deserved to go.* My sorrow is a reflection of how much I miss him, and I must say it has not gotten any better.

My sorrow manifested itself in crying spells, first only now and then, but lately they have been so unpredictable that I have stopped letting Bev stay overnight. Although she has yet to mention it, I know that Bev thinks something is up between us, but how do you tell the woman that you love that you are a crybaby? I wished I could explain to her that beyond this cool, calm, collective persona there is an emotionally scarred man who just wants to be held by her. I know that people say that women dig men who can express their emotions, but I am just not feeling it. Being that open exposes a part of me that I am not yet ready to reveal. My embarrassment over my behavior has forced me to look deeper into myself, resulting in opening myself up to new experiences of exploration so that I can find the answers for myself. Unknown to Bev and others, I'm now in therapy to deal with my grief and other matters. I realized that to get my feelings under control, I had no other choice.

I received a referral from my primary doctor to see a therapist who specializes in grief therapy. About six weeks later, as I sat filling out the numerous forms in the therapist's office, I started to feel anxious, wondering what would happen if any of my people found out about this visit. Fortunately, my anxiety morphed to surprise when I met my therapist for the first time. First of all, she was a woman, which was a shocker to me since I assumed that with a first name of Imani she would be a he, and a black he at that. My therapist was Dr. Bria: a striking redhead from Chicago who did not seem to detect my surprise in meeting her.

After introductions, she listened to my reasons for seeking therapy, asked a couple of questions, and then asked me if I had any questions.

I said, "Yes, I have one. What does a white female psychologist know about the struggles of a thirty-year-old black male?"

Dr. Bria looked over her glasses, crossed her legs, and said, "The elements of struggle are the same no matter what ethnicity, sex, or age you are. Always remember people are more alike than different. Do you really think that your blackness or your gender makes your life experiences that unique, or are you really just saying you do not think that I'm a good fit for you as a therapist, because all you see are my color and gender?"

Her response took me by surprise, and I had to think fast. *Bright woman,* I thought. Over the last week, my mental situation had gone from bad to worse, and I needed help. Remembering something from my psychology class, I stated, "I do believe that culture is an important factor to consider when assessing someone's behavior. Without an understanding of a person's culture, something may be missed, and since I do think that culturally we are different, therefore—"

But before I could say another word, Dr. Bria cut me off, saying, "Excuse me, Mr. Turner. Let me first say that today has not been a good day for me. My cat ran away, I got caught in the rain, and a person who has never landed eyes on me before is judging my therapeutic abilities. What I am about to say to you might be quite unprofessional, but I think it needs to be said, and your reaction to what I am about to say will determine if we will be working together. I am hearing you say that since we do not share the same ethnic heritage I may not be any help to you. Before you leave my office, let me tell you something. It should not factor into your decision-making but it may prevent you in the future from judging a book by its cover. I am a child of an interracial marriage: my mother is black and my father is Irish. My father left my mother when I was four, and I was raised on the south side of Chicago, a product of public housing. I am pretty sure that your cultural experience may be different than mine my brother. I'm the one who has the doubts about you, but I think that if we work together, you will be able to resolve your conflicts. So I am willing to do this on a trial basis if you are."

I was spellbound; few people had ever spoken to me in that manner, with the exception of my parents. Thus began my therapeutic relationship with Dr. Bria. Fortunately for her, I have a weakness for redheaded women with cleavage, or the therapy experiment would have been short-lived. Astonishingly, our weekly sessions did increase my understanding of my inner workings of why I do what I do. For the first time in my life, I was able to disclose to someone about what ails me, which would have been a very scary situation for me in the past.

In a recent session, Dr. Bria asked me what father's death meant to me. I replied that I viewed Dad's death as God's final judgment over his life. It had surprised me that a man so full of life one day was the next day no longer around. I could not comprehend the meaning of his death—as if a person's death even has meaning. She explained to me while I was unsuccessfully wrestling with the why part of my father's death that my emotions demanded a share of my time too. I remarked that I believe that the shock of his death had seared my soul so deeply that I did not know how to express my loss; therefore, the highly educated stupid me did what I had been taught. Being raised a Turner man, I understood exactly what to do; there would be no public expression of emotions for me. My brothers and I were taught that outward expressions of emotion might reflect negatively on an individual, so when possible, avoid those types of personal manifestations and emotions.

Yep. That is one of the many things that the old man told us boys during a Breakfast of Warriors. I remember like it was yesterday. He said, "Never let everyone know what you are feeling, because they may use it against you in the future. If you are hurting, resist the feeling; if you are ecstatic, do not show it. A calm outward expression will profit you more in the long run than a true expression of emotions."

I know that those statements were my father's attempt to prepare his sons for our future emotional battles in life. Thus, we became a closed book to anyone who attempted to elicit a true emotional response from us. Everyone, that is, but Daniel. He is different: Daniel cried at the funeral, the only one of us. Yes, he cried while we stood motionless, unwilling to connect with our feelings, or maybe not really knowing how to express that what we felt. I do not know who Dad would have been prouder of—the three stooges or Daniel. In a way, I think it would have been Daniel, because he was able to see the weakness in Dad's point of view. That point of view only worked for those who care what other people think about them. In my big brother's case, he does not care, so in a way, I see him as being much freer than his brothers.

It appears that my psychology studies had paid off because Dr. Bria was surprised about the insight that I had about my behavior, and she pushed me harder to identify more illogical thought patterns. Being trained in cognitive behavioral therapy, Dr. Bria would always say, "Remember we behave as we think. Sometimes we are dancing to old songs and we need to change the song."

One of the old songs that I am still dancing to is a belief that a man stands independent of others. Yea, another one of my dad's teachings. Since my father's death, I have come to believe that I do not have anyone in my life that I can trust to accept me for who I am. His death screwed me up—nothing so personal had ever happened to me before. I had never felt hurt like this, so whom do you go to when your soul cries out? My significant other? Well, Bev is cool, but I do not want to appear weak and fragile around her. The truth is I am fearful of her reaction. Family is out of the question; my mom would attempt to baby me while at the same time feel sorry for me. My brothers have the same dilemma as me. Friends—well, they are assholes and also scared of their emotional expressions. So my therapy continues.

My God, Jamie is still standing there with that silly "Why did I say that?" look on his face.

Chapter 11

Unknown Truths

Before Jamie could say another word, Willie moved quickly toward him and said, "Asshole, what do you mean that you did not like them? You always had difficulty facing the truth and admitting your feelings. You did not like the breakfasts? You are an asshole. Who are you trying to kid? During all of those breakfasts, you didn't even have to wait like the rest of us to order. Because you were the oldest, Daddy let you order first. I hated that, and now you going to say that you did not enjoy the breakfasts? I'll kick your ass."

Surprisingly, Willie's comeback did not seem to faze Jamie. He just turned and went back to hoeing that row. After a couple of minutes, he turned back to face his brothers. Willie, Daniel, and Rob Jr. had surrounded him by now. Jamie looked up, smiling, and said, "What I'm about to say I have never told anyone, not even my wife. All I ask you guys to do is listen and do not comment on what I say until after I'm finished. Agreed?"

Daniel looked at Willie and Rob Jr. They stood silently with pissed looks on their faces. Reluctantly, the three nodded their approval.

Jamie started, "You guys truly believe being the oldest in that house while living with your mother and father was an easy task. Well, it was not. Being made to be the example, not free to make a mistake, and feeling the weight of the family on your shoulders made me crazy. I am the eldest Turner male; my assigned role was to set the example for my younger brothers to follow. You are right: I enjoyed the attention I received at the breakfasts. But at the same time, I hated it. I could not be myself; I had to be what Daddy viewed as correct. It was like I was sacrificing myself for Ma and Dad. I wanted to go away for college, but I stayed close to home and attended Cleveland State so that it would not place such a financial a burden on the family. No regrets. I received a good education, although I commuted from home. After graduation I had an opportunity to start a job in Atlanta, but I didn't. Dad had just retired, and with his money flow reduced, he asked me to stay around to assist with you guys in going to college. Again, no regrets. I found me a good job, a wonderful wife, but if I had my druthers, I would have been in Atlanta."

Jamie turned his eyes toward Willie, his voice tense. "When one of you assholes got kicked out of college, that nearly killed Daddy. Because it was me, not Daddy, who financed your education. Yea, I know you were on a baseball scholarship, but it did not cover all your expenses so I picked up the rest. Why? Because he asked me to, so I did it. He told me how much and I gave it him, no questions, no regrets. Would I have done it on my own? Hell no, because I knew something that our father didn't. He believed in you, but I knew you were not ready for college. He was proud of your accomplishments in baseball. Oh yea, you would always hear him say how Willie did this and Willie did that. He was your biggest cheerleader, but he was blind to your deficits. When you dropped out of school, it broke his heart. He would have never told you. That was not his way. Busted knee my ass. Just busted pride."

Willie looked away, not able to face his brother.

Jamie then turned his focus to Daniel. "By the time you had left for Philly, Rob Jr. was finishing up high school. Daddy knew that you would not need his help; you were not raised like that. Dad allowed you to be the verbally expressive one. He wanted to see how long you would kick against the prick. So he let you, Daniel, be argumentative with Ma. He thought that Ma would win, but you surprised him. You did not let Ma wear you down. You did everything that you could to upset Ma, especially your interest in white women, which even shocked Dad."

Daniel just looked at Jamie with no emotion. Jamie appeared a little tired, but continued on. "By the time Rob Jr. was old enough for college, Dad had given him over to Ma. He had taken three from her, so he thought that she deserved a keeper. You guys may wonder how I know so much. Well, Dad talked to me. While you all were playing baseball, chasing white women, and just doing stupid things, I was sitting across the street on that porch, listening, nodding, and smiling at Dad. When you two idiots found time from your misadventures, you all came back home, with the exception of Daniel, who is an idiot."

Willie yelled, "I tired of listening to this bull crap!"

"Hey, Willie, let him finish."

"He better hurry up."

From across the street, the brothers heard a familiar voice. "Daniel, what you boys doing? Is it break time already? You planted those tomatoes too close to that fence again, Daniel. What were you thinking? And Willie, what the hell are you doing over there raising your voice? You don't want me to come across this street, do you?"

"No, ma'am."

"Well, then, lower your voice and get some darn work done. Boy, you sure are lazy."

"Yes, ma'am."

The voice temporarily brought calm back to the garden. The brothers scattered, resuming their duties without further fanfare or conversation. Willie mumbled to himself as he picked up some carrot seeds, "This ain't over. Who the hell he thinks he is? Damn mama's boy."

Rob Jr. picked up some cabbage plants and put them in the wheelbarrow. Although he was awaiting direction, Rob Jr. could tell by his brothers' faces that everyone, for the moment, had escaped to their own worlds and the command of what to do would not be coming anytime soon. Jamie's perception of their childhood had given each of them something to think about. He was not surprised by Willie's reaction, because he knew his brother pretty well. After Willie did not return to college, he changed—became lost. Getting kicked out of school was a difficult thing for Willie to swallow, since he had never been cut from any team in his life. Rob Jr.'s relationship with his older brother suffered.

Daniel moved toward the fence to see what his mother was talking about. *Too close? There are at least two feet between the fence and this row. I think Ma is going loony. or she's back to her old ways of seeking attention.*

Daniel turned back to assess the garden's progress. Although all of the seeds and plants had not yet been planted, and not all of the rubbish had been removed, he still felt like a proud father. Where there was nothing but a couple of baby cabbage and tomato plants, Daniel foresaw of a plentiful autumn harvest of beans, cabbage, tomatoes, peppers, and greens.

The garden's transformation from nothing into something reminded Daniel of his own journey into manhood. Growing up, his family saw him as a scrawny pain in the ass. Through careful cultivation and fertilization, not unlike that which occurs in a garden, Daniel had developed into a Turner man. In Daniel's day, becoming a man was equated with reaching the age of twenty-one. At the age of twenty-one, qualities that were supposed to be developed, such as responsibility and a work ethic, would equip a male for manhood. It was Daniel's belief that for certain individuals, the concept of responsibility would never be fully acquired, and thus many males enter manhood ill prepared for its rigor.

Daniel certainly did not lack a sense of responsibility. In the Turner household, responsibility is one of the tenants that a child learns early in life, or else he paid the consequences. Since the payment came in human flesh, the Turner boys were known to be the responsible type, with the exception of Willie. Not surprisingly, Daniel's journey to manhood was quite the opposite—and delayed.

Instead of being elevated into manhood at the age of twenty-one, he was subjected to a more intense, prolonged initiation process. The one thing that Daniel's life experiences had not fostered in him was a sense of humility. The Turners' parenting style was rich in lessons of pride and self-esteem but void of instructions on being humble. It would not be until life's events beat him down, causing him to cry out to his God, that Daniel would fully step into manhood. Therefore, becoming a man was a humbling experience for Daniel, seasoned with the understanding that without God in his life, he could do nothing. At the age of thirty-three, when that crowning moment arrived, Daniel knew that he had become a man and everything would be different now. As he looked around, watching his brothers at their tasks, he shook his head and thought, *Farmers we are not.*

Daniel yelled out, "Willie, what the hetch are you doing?"

"I'm resting. You know that my old baseball injury gives me problems every now and then."

"So your knee is still bothering you after all these years?"

"Big brother, my knee always bothers me. It's like it was just yesterday. One day I was headed down the ski slopes in New York, the next day I'm lying in the operating room."

"Not the story of your fall from grace again!" yelled Rob Jr.

The brothers howled in laughter. Finally, Willie was the butt of a joke.

"Laugh, you fools. I was this close to greatness, and you all know it," stated Willie as he picked up some containers of peppers to plant.

"Yes, you were great—in your own mind," replied Rob Jr., and another round of laughter ensued.

Surprisingly, Willie did not respond but continued to inspect the peppers, while all the time thinking that his brothers were just jealous of what could have been.

CHAPTER 12

Willie

Yes, I had it all. Could have written my own ticket, but I screwed up. Yep, I did. It started with a freaking phone call.

"Skiing, hmm … I would love to. No, I never have before, but how difficult can it be?"

The phone call, the question, and what occurred afterward would become a turning point in my life. The phone call was from Paulette, my newest love interest at the time. I was home on Christmas break during my junior year at Ohio University. College was the bomb for me. I was on my way to becoming a bona fide professional baseball prospect, getting well known around campus, and loving it. After batting .385 during my junior year baseball season, I was voted the all-conference centerfielder for the second year in a row. I was hot, especially with the women. Or at least I thought so any way. A group of students from OU were going skiing and Paulette asked me if I would join them.

Upon hearing about this, Garland "Little Man" Walker, my college roommate who would later stand in the hospital lobby shaking his head as they rolled me past him, warned me against going. "Skiing is a sport for white folks, and you ain't white."

I laughed at him and said, "Little Man, don't worry. I'm a warrior, son of Helena and Robert, child of a king. Those mere facts should keep me safe from danger."

"Whatever," he replied.

What I can remember from the skiing trip that I have not repressed is that I fell, it hurt, I could not get up, and it was cold. Others would say that I looked fabulous until I ran into that tree. "What tree?" I would later ask. Others would often ask me, "What the hell were you doing skiing?" This question was asked several times by my parents, my roommate, and especially my coach. If I had told them that the real reason I went skiing was to impress a young lady, I probably would have fared better in some people's eyes. But to save face, I lied. I told everyone I did it on a dare. As a result of the lie, I was looked down on as a pitiful fool who allowed his dreams to be dashed because of having too much pride and not enough common sense—a terrible paring of stupidity.

I can remember being wheeled into a room and hearing muted voices all around me. The room smelled sterile—the type of hospital antiseptic scent that assaults your nostrils. There was a clock somewhere close by just ticking. I remember a group of masked individuals surrounding my bed. The bed sheet covering my lower body was removed, and there was silence, like a million sharply trained minds were working quietly.

Then one of the masked individuals spoke. "Tell me again what happened."

"A skiing accident ... mmm."

"Where are the X-rays?"

More silence as someone turned on a light board with several X-rays of my knee displayed.

"Well, I don't think he will be doing that again for a while."

I later learned the voice belonged to Dr. Roesch, an orthopedic surgeon who performed surgery on my right knee. I knew from the tone of her voice that I was fucked. Dr. Roesch told me to look up, and I was slow to respond as she asked me a couple of questions while looking at my eyes. I smiled, trying to answer the questions as best as I could, at the same time thinking that she was a beautiful woman. Another voice off to the right of my head woke me up from my doctor-patient fantasy and told me to begin counting backward from one hundred as they placed some type of mask over my face. That is all I can remember about the operation.

I woke up in a very cold room trying to remember how the hell I got there and where my angel I dreamed about was. In the distance, I heard voices again coming toward me. I felt lightheaded and everything was a blur. A glow appeared, and I heard the angel's voice. She congratulated me on coming through the surgery. I attempted to smile but did not have much control over my facial muscles.

With my consciousness slowly leaving me, my angel made the following statement: "You will require extensive rehabilitation to walk again, but with hard work you, should be fine."

To walk again? The words reverberated in my mind over and over. What was my angel saying? Everything was spinning and becoming more blurred. *To walk again?* I internally yelled in my pain-pill-induced state. But it was to no avail as I slipped into the unconscious world of no pain, experiencing my mind and what I perceived as the truth colliding.

But this is the middle point of my story. Let's start from the beginning so that all of this can make some sense. I must agree that school was never my thing. It was not that I lacked the ability to learn; it was the motivational piece that was in short supply for me. Like one coach after another told me, "Boy, it is not your skill level that will make you great. It's the application of those skills."

Yes, I did lack application when it came to my schoolwork. I could do it; I just didn't. That lack of application would come back to haunt me sooner rather than later. It was not until I took a liking to baseball that my world began to make sense to me. Baseball at that time was America's favorite pastime. In theory, it's quite a simple game. Someone throws a ball, someone tries to hit the ball, and someone tries to catch the ball. So simple, yet so difficult.

My baseball career began in the backyard when I was about five years old, but it really began to blossom at Dupont Park. Dupont was the name of the park that was around the corner from my house. It housed two baseball fields with lights, bleachers, and a concession stand. Before the neighborhood had changed, men's fast-pitched softball teams played nightly at Dupont. But with the exodus of white families from the area, the softball leagues followed suit. Sometimes someone's loss can be another's gain. The departure of the men's softball leagues led to there being an opening for little league baseball at Dupont. Not surprisingly, all the boys in the neighborhood were okay with the loss of men's softball. I graduated from the neighborhood pick-up games directly to Big F, the older boys league, skipping Little F altogether. Although I was age eligible to play Little F baseball, my baseball skills were advanced for my age, so I was recruited by Coach Young to play centerfield for his Big F team, the Angels.

Why I was better at baseball than the other guys in the neighborhood, I cannot say. It just came naturally for me; neither hitting nor catching a baseball was ever a problem. While I was achieving success in baseball, my status in the family was changing. Right when my baseball glory was bringing me attention in the neighborhood, the birth of Rob Jr. was sucking away all my possible positive attention in the family. My poor school achievement only further sustained my family's negative attention, which my simple-minded brothers enjoyed to no end. My relationship with my siblings at this point was normal, in a Turner type of way. I ignored my younger brother and plotted against my two older ones. One of the capers that I masterminded, which I now truly regret, was the death of Jamie's goldfish, Alicia.

You see, pets in the Turner family were a no-no. Although my parents never stated their reasons for not allowing pets in the house, my dad's rationale most likely was truly economical, as he saw pets as something else to feed, while my mother's reasoning was emotional, as pets most likely reminded her of the south, which she despised. Come to think of it, anything negative reminded Mama of her southern upbringing. So for Jamie to get permission to have a pet was a big thing in my family, or maybe just to me. As an envious younger sibling, I sought to bring Jamie to his knees, no matter the cost. I even included Daniel in the plan. I told him that I was doing a scientific project to determine if Alicia, Jamie's fish, could exist in saltwater. I needed him to truly believe that I was doing a science project in case I got caught; he would be my witness that I was doing it for school and not out of spite. So one day, I did it. I poured salt into the fish bowl. Just a little at first, and then I pretended to stumble, pouring a whole bunch into the bowl. It was not long before Alicia bellied up. Daniel jumped up and down and said, "Willie, look what you have done. Jamie is going to kill you."

As soon as the salt entered into the bowl, I knew that I was doing something wrong, but I could not stop. Alicia's death was quick, a couple of bubbles, a wave of the fins, and then silence as she floated on top of the water. Daniel and I nearly shit in our pants, and everything after that is a blur to me, except how Jamie handled her death. You would have thought that Alicia was his girlfriend the way he moped around. It took the loss of someone close to me to occur before I understood what Jamie must have felt that day about Alicia.

My stupid prank on his fish intensified the negativity in our already less-than-great relationship. He stopped talking to Daniel and me, and if he passed me, he'd always give me that "I'm going to fuck you up look." Jamie became moodier, more distant, and was a pain to be around. My father surprisingly offered to replace Alicia with another fish, but Jamie refused. He emphasized that the death of someone or something (in Jamie's case) close to you can be an irreplaceable loss. I truly believe that Jamie has systematically sought out his revenge on my brother and me. Since the fish incident, strange accidents or disappearances have occurred in the house. Too many to talk about, but I am sure that Jamie is the mastermind behind those occurrences, although he has continued to deny it.

Well, that's all about Jamie and his crazy fish. After a questionable junior high experience, I attended Glenville High School, where I starred on the baseball team. We were city champs my senior year but lost in the semifinal of the state tournament. I was the school's first all-state baseball player and received a full scholarship from Ohio University. Academically, my work in the classroom was not as stellar, but I passed with some tutoring help from my younger brother, who continues to remind me of it until this day.

Like at Glenville, baseball at Ohio University was easy, but I struggled academically my first year until I began receiving support from an unlikely source: my white female co-eds. Truth be told, from my sophomore year on, I never wrote a paper and received assistance on every test or exam I took. I hit .389 my freshman year while playing centerfield every game, a first for a freshman at OU. I soon discovered some of the perks of being a full scholarship player at a major university. Known only to my roommate Little Man, I kept regular company with a handful of "forbidden fruits," as my Uncle Sonny called them, during my time at OU.

Life was good and on the verge of getting better until a series of bad decisions caused my downward spiral. My friend Fast Eddy once said, "Behind every man's bad decision, there lies a woman somewhere." In my case, I am a witness, a victim, and a full participant. I do not know why I said yes. Maybe it was that black dress I saw her in or—hmm, yes I do know—I wanted her. I was scared to go skiing, but I had to go through with it because of this Turner thing of being a man of your word. Yea, my father—I can blame all of this on him and those damn Warrior talks. I had internalized all the stuff that he taught us about being a man. One of his major tenets was the belief that a Turner man is a man of his word. Well, since I told Paulette that I was going, I had to go, because if I was not going, I should have told her that—because I am a man, and a man is only as good as his word. I believe that was Warrior talk number 12. It is kinda funny how Daddy numbered his talks with us, even funnier that I remember the numbers. It is amazing how much of an effect my father had on how we thought and behaved. He was always in our heads, even more now than when he was around. You can hear him saying, "A Turner man this. A Turner man that."

His voice was always there directing, commenting, and suggesting. Just like the superego I that read about in intro psychology class, his way always represented the higher moral path. I guess Freud was right—about that point anyway.

Bad decision number one: yes I, Willie Turner, all-star centerfielder for the Ohio University baseball team, traveled to the state of New York in an attempt to impress a young lady by going skiing, though I had never desired, thought about, or considered going skiing until she asked me. Motivated by ego and lust, I unfortunately landed in the hospital with a torn knee ligament, which according to my angel doctor meant I faced at least a year of rehab.

Bad decision number two: I eventually stopped going to class after the skiing incident. It was the natural reaction of an asshole. After being hollered at by my parents, friends, and all of my coaches, I was a little down and embarrassed. My knee hurt and so did my pride, so to avoid my peers, I dropped a couple of classes and hid out in the trainer room. I stopped going to all of my classes by the next semester—heck I had batted .389, I thought I deserved a break or two. We had won the conference, we were champs, it was time to party, and party I did, causing me to miss a couple of final exams. The victors go the spoils, and I was attempting to suck up the spoils all in one gulp.

My knee was not sturdy enough to begin baseball spring training—no surprise given that I could not even run without it hurting. Every time I was going for a jog, just a darn jog, the knee would swell up. By the beginning of spring semester, nobody was talking to me except for Little Man. My coaches avoided me after they found out that my knee had not healed. When they did see me in the trainer's room, they gave me lukewarm support saying crap like "Hanging in there, we can't wait to get you back," though they were probably thinking, *You Idiot, how can you be so dumb? You had the world by its balls.* So baseball season came and went without me. Since I was unable to play, I was declared medically ineligible for the season, which allowed me to have three years of eligibility left. It was the first time in my life that I did not start or even get into a game all season. My angel doctor was correct when she said that my knee would require extensive rehabilitation, but she forgot to inform me that rehab would be painful. Suddenly, college was not any fun anymore. Crazy thoughts began to flood my mind. Although I joked and laughed with the guys, I started to think that they were laughing at me, and not with me, so I gradually removed myself from their company and became a loner. My party boy image disintegrated as quickly as it appeared. My paranoia spread beyond my social group. I thought my professors were involved in a conspiracy against me, so I stayed away from my classes because I did not want to be perceived as a failure and be taunted by them for not being prepared for class. Baseball had been my shield from the world—it had allowed me to elevate myself over most people because I had something special that people honored. I was a winner. But now that it was gone, at least for the moment, I felt unprotected, anxious, and vulnerable. I saw my world becoming smaller and smaller. When I walked down the street, I felt the eyes of by passers following my every movement, questioning my existence, and second-guessing my motives. I began to think … maybe my coaches, professors and peers will see that I really do not belong in college—it was baseball, not smarts that got me as far as I had gotten. I began comparing my situation with that of a winning thoroughbred horse that had become lame, but going out to pasture to become a stud is probably not what is planned for my future. What would they do with me? Well, that question was soon answered. That answer came in a white envelope from the college Department of Registrar, and it had more to do with me than with them.

My second mistake resulted in me being academically ineligible. Due to the mental state that I was in at the time, being sent home was probably the best thing for me. Saying good-bye to my coaches and friends was easy; I just continued to avoid them. When the semester ended, I packed up my boxes and rode out of town with Little Man. I had no regrets at that time about the way I left, my paranoid mind had forced me to become a hermit, and I knew it was time to go, with or without good-byes. It is a funny thing about men—we never know how to say what we want to say when we need to say something. Instead of telling Little Man how appreciative I was of his support, I just said, "Thanks man, I will be in touch." We shook hands, and he drove off. Yea, I said thanks, but for what? For the ride home, or for his support? I wish sometimes I had the courage to say the words that needed to be said when they needed to be said, but remember I am a man.

By going home I thought that I could regroup, get my head straight, take some classes at Cleveland State, get my average back up, and return to OU in the spring, eligible to return to baseball. Well, those were good thoughts and ideas, but like I mentioned before, I have very bad application. Although I had good intentions, mentally I was still paranoid, and spiritually, I was broken knowing I had disappointed my father. A normal individual who was wounded and mentally unstable would return home and seek the love of their family and my friends to help them through this rough period of their life, but not a Turner man.

Telling my family that I was not going back to school was not as bad as waiting for their reactions. My brothers Jamie and Robert just sat there with dumb looks on their faces when I announced my decision to stay home. Daniel was away somewhere in Europe, therefore he missed the circus. It was like they were reacting to the news in slow motion. But I was not surprised, I knew that they would react with indifference and wait for our parents' reaction. We were raised to be individuals who stood their own ground. My situation would not be their concern, and with my paranoia kicking in, I perceived it may be to their benefit. With my status in the family dropping, my brothers might attempt to capitalize on the moment. Furthermore, knowing my brothers like I do, they would use it against me in the future. My parents' reaction was another matter. My mother, with her dramatic self, was the first one to speak. She said, "The only thing those coaches wanted to do is to use Willie for their own purposes. I'm so happy that you are home Willie, you look so thin. Eat, boy."

I think Mom's real reason for relief was that because I was back home, I would not be chasing any of that forbidden fruit I spoke of earlier. My father's reaction was more subtle. He asked me one question and made one statement. He asked, "So what are your plans?"

So I laid out my goals for the next year and how I expected to accomplish them. Then he said, "Since you are back living here, don't forget that the garbage goes out on Tuesday."

With that statement, my father finished his potatoes, drank the rest of his iced tea, and went into the living room to watch the evening news. It was not that I was surprised by his reaction, but I didn't know if his mention of the garbage was a reference to me, or if he really wanted me to put out the garbage on Tuesday.

Fast-forward one year, and my anxiety has disappeared, my educational plan has stalled, and I am working at the Post Office. I am now someone's husband and about to become a father. None of this was according to the plan—I guess something went dramatically wrong. Well, let us take the easy things first. Since I had to support myself, I put in an application at the Post Office and got hired. It was a big moment for me. It was the first time in my life that I believed I had received something based on skills other than baseball. When I told my father the news, he smiled and said, "Good to hear that ... Well, since you are working, don't forget to give your mother some money for rent ... Welcome to my world."

"Yes, sir."

Surprisingly, my father never mentioned baseball or my plan for going back to school. I did take a couple of classes at Cleveland State, but my old nemesis—lack of application—came along to haunt me.

I missed some classes and found myself behind, so I dropped both classes and took on more overtime at work. I guess what they say is true: college is not for everyone. As I continued to work out the demons in my head, I was reintroduced to someone from my past, a high school friend named Deitra Brown. Circumstances and my poor decision making made me prime for what happened next. My academic failures and my perceived loss of my father's love had me feeling like crap about myself. I could deal with me not being a good student, heck I knew that all along, but the loss of my father's love was hard to swallow. After I dropped the classes at Cleveland State, I began avoiding him, not wanting him to ask about how well I was working my plan. I was scared of being viewed by him as a total failure. Suddenly, without baseball, I felt like a nobody, with nothing. That was until Deitra came into my life.

Like everyone, I desired attention, and Deitra gave it to me without asking about baseball. Her love allowed me to slowly build up my self-esteem and become reconnected to life. I felt good about myself for the first time in a while, my paranoia ghosts had even deserted me, and life was good. I find that relationships are illogical things due to that two individuals are creating a union while attempting to keep their individuality. The union that Deitra and I created was workable for a while, and the attention was good for me. One day Deitra told me that she had missed her period for the last three months and had been sick to her stomach a lot lately. A trip to the free clinic the next day revealed what we already knew: she was three months pregnant. To her credit, Deitra had the ability to see the good side to any situation. While she appeared ecstatic about being pregnant with our child, I only foresaw doom and gloom. Deitra was happy about being pregnant, and I wanted to support her, but I really did not know what to say because I did not feel the same way. But a funny thing happened ... I tried to look at life through her eyes. You see, after Deitra finished high school, she attended community college and graduated with an Associate's Degree in graphic design. Soon thereafter, she got a fulltime job at Kelso Advertising Agency and moved out of her parents' house. She is quite the independent type and our chance meeting was truly a blessing for the both of us. According to Deitra, her relationship with her family was not the best; therefore my presence in her life gave her someone to love and to be loved by. So I did something that surprised even me: I confided in my father about my situation. I cannot remember the last time I asked my father for advice; it was a really scary moment. My father was sitting on the porch watching the goings-on in the street. I sat next to him on the glider and blurted out quickly,

"Dad, I need some advice. Deitra is pregnant." "Deitra, who's that?"

"My girlfriend."

"That little girl pregnant? … Hmm, how many months?" "Three going on four."

"So what advice do you need?" "I'm confused about what to do." "Are you confused or scared?"

"Probably scared more than anything else." "What does she want?"

"She is happy about the pregnancy."

"Well, there's your answer. Do the right thing, and do it quickly." "Yes, sir."

I could not figure out if he was surprised or upset about our conversation. But I knew what I had to do. The conversation took me to another level of manhood. My father's advice to me was quite simple—one of the many things he had taught his sons was that there are many choices in life and to always take the higher road. So I did—I asked Deitra to marry me, she agreed, and we became husband and wife in the fifth month of her pregnancy with my child. Yes, I did say marriage and child in the same sentence. Marriage, yes. That's what I thought was the right thing to do. During Sunday dinner when I told my family about my upcoming marriage to Deitra, the typical behaviors occurred: my brothers became mute, my mother nearly fainted, and Dad said, "Good luck," and continued to eat his dinner. Thus, the Turner way.

The following weekend I informed my parents that I was moving in with Deitra until we got married. As I packed my boxes, my father came up to my bedroom and just looked at me. After what seemed like ages, he said, "Willie, I can't say that I foreseen this coming in your life, although I'm not surprised. How a person progresses through life is based on the decisions they make along the way. One decision can make you go left, while another one can make you go right. Being a man has to do with becoming responsible for the decisions you make in your life. Understandably, your mother is quite upset with you, but you know that. In the envelope is a type of support that you may need if you are going to have a family."

He gave me an envelope with five hundred dollars in it, shook my hand, and left. Two weeks later, Deitra and I got married in a simple ceremony at Cleveland City Hall, along with about two dozen other scared individuals. It was a happy moment for us. After the ceremony we went to lunch and took in a movie. During the movie, Deitra whispered in my ear that she found out yesterday from her doctor that she is having twins. The news sent shockwaves through my body, forcing me to pull her closer to me, not in a gesture of love, but for stability. My heart began to pound but I forced myself to look her straight in the eyes with a smile from ear to ear and say, "Oh baby!" while praying silently, *Oh my God, please help us.*

Unfortunately, for reasons unknown, God did not grant my request, and Deitra lost the twins. She had a miscarriage in the seventh month of her pregnancy due to unforeseen medical complications. Only two months into our marriage, the death angel's unannounced appearance ultimately set off the beginning of the end for us. It was not a good time for us, though I'm sure there is never a good time for the death of your unborn children. If our relationship consisted of two healthy individuals, we might have been able to withstand such a difficult blow, but we were two broken individuals from the start who needed each other to stand up straight. The deaths sucked the life out of us. I did not how to comfort her, and she did not know how to accept comfort. How do you comfort a mother who has lost her child, and in our case, two children? How do you comfort yourself about your own loss? Who comforts you? Too many questions for a young couple to answer. Family and friends … well those friends who knew that she was pregnant were invisible and non-supportive … and my family went into self-induced amnesia. The weight of the situation caused cracks to appear in our relationship. Internal blame created external quietness, minds engaged on the reason of why, while the present needs of themselves and the other went unattended.

I never had a strong belief in God, and surprisingly it was not the death of the twins but seeing how Deitra suffered that made me question the existence of a just God. My soul cried out daily for an explanation of why someone as sweet and wonderful as my wife had to experience such a heavy burden. The expected non-response from my God sent me into a downward spiral where I saw nothing good about life or living. Though my thoughts were never suicidal, life had lost its joy for me. My baby was hurting and there was nothing I could do about it. The very seeds of my loins were gone before they even came, and I was left grieving about what could have been. What do you do when you do not know what to do? Being young and dumb did not help. Instead of seeking professional help for my wife and myself, which was probably the right thing to do, I did nothing because I did not know what was the right thing to do. There were no great solutions given by those around us who found it to be their business to give us advice.

"Give it time."

"Get back on that horse again."

"You guys are young, you have plenty of more chances."

Stupid advice from stupid people who say stupid things.

I cannot say that the distance between Deitra and I widened, we just never reconnected. The "we" had been torn apart, leaving two hurt individuals. The emotional trauma that emerged as a result of the miscarriage caused us to lose the belief that we, as a couple, could make it through whatever we had to face. Internally, we felt that we had failed ourselves, and more importantly, failed each other. It is easy to deal with failure to one's self, but to feel that you have disappointed the one you love—that is heavy. We were scared to fail each other again; therefore, we never reconnected. We continued to exist as individuals, and the "we" of being a couple was gone.

Over time, my learned helplessness began to dissolve and I started to focus on the mess that I had left untouched. I had just begun to re-examine my relationship with my God, my wife, and my family when Deitra requested a divorce. Just like that, my time was up. I was in the living room reading the newspaper when she said in her quiet voice,

"We—no, I can't do this anymore. It hurts too much …
I have to go."

To save herself, Deitra believed she had to end the relationship, walk away, and start anew. Her statement left me speechless—just the other day we had talked about possibly going on vacation. I just sat there, trying to process what had just happened. A lump appeared in my throat, tears quickly formed, and I started to shake. I could not hold it together—so I wept. I wept for the loss of my wife, I wept for the loss of my marriage, I wept for the loss of my children, and I wept for the loss of my baseball career. I wept for everything that I had allowed to roll over my back in the past, simply because I was a Turner man. My tolerance bag had finally burst, and there was an emotional payment due for all the hurt I had suppressed. Deitra sat quietly across from me, watching. I think she understood what was happening inside of me. She was often surprised by my non-reactions to different situations in life. What she did not know is that each hurtful situation was deposited in my emotional tolerance bag, where they quietly stayed until the bag was filled and burst, and today was that day. So she sat besides me, somehow knowing there was no comfort that she could give, and that each tear that flowed down my face had meaning and any attempt to wipe them away would diminish my hurt. After what seemed like forever, I stopped and said, "I'm sorry … I'm just so sorry … you did not need to see that."

"I'm still your wife, so thank you for sharing yourself with me. But baby, what I said was not meant to hurt you, but to save you … We tried, we tried hard, but life beat us back, so we need to stop blaming ourselves. There is just too much hurt and it has consumed us. It's time for me to go."

With those words, my wife of twenty months gave me a kiss on the head and walked out of my life. She left to save herself—simply being with me everyday did not allow her to release her pain so that she could heal. Seeing my face daily, sharing the same space as me, being haunted by what could have been but was not—it all became emotionally unhealthy because no healing was occurring; we were merely making vain attempts to deal with the present. Although I was emotionally distraught over the events of the day, in a crazy way I was relieved that it was over. I know that I did not have enough of whatever we needed to go forward. Those last eighteen months had taken a toll on me. I could repress my grief, but not being able to protect my wife from the hurt had sucked the marrow from my bones. I had never felt so impotent in my life.

One month later I moved back into my room at the Turner House. My mother was elated, but my father avoided me, or I avoided him. Then one day everything changed, because he died.

Chapter 13

The Fire

Over the next five hours the lot went from being a barren piece of ground to a decent looking garden, despite a couple of disagreements over who should do what, along with an ill-advised water fight started by Willie. No one can ever say that the Turner men worked as an efficient unit. It was more like four independent workers brought together to complete a job under the guidance of a general contractor, Mrs. Turner. Each son had their assignment, although Daniel operated like the foreman of the bunch, but make no mistake, all orders came from the porch. Daniel's role was to relay his mother's wishes for the garden to the brothers. This sometimes placed Daniel in hot water, especially when it came to the mulberry tree.

The garden's mulberry tree grew from a cutting off the tree that was in the backyard of Mrs. Turner parents' home. Yep, the same tree that Mrs. Turner's father was found dead under. How the tree, or a cutting from the tree, got all the way to Cleveland, Ohio is an interesting tale. There was a series of occurrences that happened down south that had a direct bearing on the tree's existence in the garden. First, the year after the death of the boys' grandfather, the mulberry tree stopped bearing fruit. The tree would bloom in the spring, but nary a berry would appear in the summer. A scientifically minded person might postulate that the reason that the tree was barren was due to an infestation of worms, or maybe the bees were at fault for not pollinating the blooms. But the mystic minded individuals, like Aunt May, had a different idea. She denounced any potential scientific reasons as gibberish, saying any fool could tell the difference between a diseased tree and one that was hurting. Aunt May believed that all living things, plants, animals, human, and even insects, had souls and therefore could experience emotions. She told everyone who would listen that the tree's fruitless state was due to all the suffering its soul had witnessed in the last couple of years. No one paid any attention to Aunt May's diagnosis—until the day of the big fire that burned down the house.

Still, to this day, no one knows how the fire started. At the time of the fire, Mrs. Turner was down south, staying at the house to attend the funeral services of her grandmother, who had recently passed. She had brought Daniel and Jamie with her, leaving the younger boys home with her husband. Going back down south was not one of Mrs. Turner's favorite things to do. But after moving to Cleveland to live with her aunt, she had promised Grandma Helena that she would come back home at least once a year to visit. But she hated it. The smells, the heat, the people, and the memories seemed to be waiting for her when she got off the bus. No matter how much Mrs. Turner had repressed the memories of her childhood, once she went south, they came rolling back. Even her southern twang of an accent met her at the bus door, welcoming her back home. After she got married, her means for transportation varied; sometimes she would drive down with Mr. Turner, and other times she would take the boys down on the Greyhound bus, and sometimes Mr. Turner would drive down to pick them up. Whatever the arrangement, it was the same old thing to her and she did not want any part of it. The death of Grandma Helena came as a shock to her, however, and the company of her two oldest children was comforting for her.

The fire started the morning after the funeral, and Mrs. Turner and the boys woke up to the smell of smoke. Luckily, Mrs. Turner had packed their suitcases the night before and had those ready downstairs for their departure the next day. Smelling smoke and seeing the flames coming from the fields in the back terrified Mrs.

Turner. She and the boys quickly grabbed their suitcases and ran out the front door, running toward the road, which was about one hundred yards from the house. By the time they got to the road, the fire had reached the back of the house and all the nearby neighbors had gathered, even Mr. Tucker. There he stood in the midst of all those black folks, wondering like they were just what in the world happened to cause such a large fire. Theories ranged from an isolated lightening strike to a homeless man's campfire that got out of control. But Ms. Dominique, who lived down the road, said that she heard something that sounded like voices … yea, voices singing. When she heard the voices, she ran to her kitchen window. She then saw the fire moving across the field toward Grandma Helena's house. With the only fire engine way off in town, nothing nor nobody could save the house. Strangely, the mulberry tree was the only thing left standing after the fire. Everything around it was burned to a crisp: the house, the fields, the shed, but not the tree. It just stood there as a reminder, darkened and charred, but still alive. While the ground was still hot, Aunt May walked over to the mulberry tree and cut off the lowest branch. She trimmed the end with her pocketknife, placed the branch in a canning jar with water, said something to the branch, and gave it to Daniel. Aunt May told Daniel to keep the branch in the jar until it rooted, and then in the fall plant the tree outside where there is plenty of light and it could be seen from their house. She explained to him later in a letter that the tree's survival was a sign, though of what, she could not yet tell. Thankfully for the family, Mr. Turner and the younger boys had arrived during the fire, and Mr. Turner could see the smoke from miles away. After some tearful good-byes, Mr. Turner scooped his family into the car, along with the tree cutting, and headed back north. Mrs. Turner cursed at Daniel for bringing the tree cutting in the car, but Mr. Turner interceded and told her to allow him to have it, and that was that. So back to Cleveland went three trauma-scarred individuals, along with a cutting from a tree that would not die. Mrs. Turner thought the cutting would never bear roots or even survive Cleveland's bitter winters. But to her surprise the cutting became a tree, and a very large one at that over the years. But it has yet to bear any fruit.

Mrs. Turner despised the tree, and every year she promised to have the darn thing cut down. The battle for the tree's survival is a fierce and somewhat comical one because Mrs. Turner will not go anywhere near the tree. She calls it the tree of death and is secretly afraid of it due it having survived the fire. She will not even allow the shade of the tree to cover her. Naw, she knows what Aunt May says is true—that the tree has a soul … and it knows suffering, like the suffering that Mrs. Turner experienced in her childhood. The tree's existence is a constant reminder to Mrs. Turner of her past. The tree knows her and from where she comes from. It is the only living witness in Cleveland who knew Mrs. Turner before she became Mrs. Turner. As the tree survived the Cleveland winters, She became more fearful that the tree would tell her neighbors the true story of her impoverished upbringing and all of the sorrows she witnessed. Yes, in her traumatized mind, the tree is a threat and it must go.

From her perch across the street on the porch, Mrs. Turner kept a constant eye on sons working in the garden, barking out instructions, directions, and encouragement as she saw fit. Everyone, except for Robert, knew before they could lay down their garden tools their beloved mother had to come across the street to inspect their work. Daniel was finishing collecting the bell pepper containers while Jamie was watering the back section of the garden. As Willie planted his last cabbage plant he looked up and saw Mrs. Turner putting on her house shoes, preparing for her trip to the garden.

"Oh shoot," said Willie. "Here she comes."

"What you talking about?" replied Robert.

"Your mother is a coming to inspect the garden and what she says determines if we can leave or not."

"Are you serious? I can't stay too much longer."

"Well, you better pray for the best, because you know how your Mama can be."

Yes, indeed, Robert has experienced his mother's pickiness, just like the rest of his brothers. He can remember once how she made him refold all the towels in the linen closet because he forgot to turn the fold of the towel toward the right side. *But not today Mama,* thought Robert, *I need to be somewhere else soon, and time is not on my side.* He was still unsure what he would say; the whole situation was more than he could have imagined. *Me, a possible father, wow ...* Robert began to think deeply on the meaning of those words. The thought crisscrossed Robert's mind so many times that it made him dizzy. He stumbled and grasped the fence for support. Unfortunately for Robert, his stumble was observed by Willie.

"You okay?" Willie asked as he walked toward him.
"You don't look so good ... it's only your mother coming. I think you better sit down, here sit here in this chair ... Anyway she has stop to talk to Mrs. Bray, so we are good for another fifteen minutes or so ... Daniel, throw me one of those bottles of water over here ... I think we done working, Robert here close to his death."

Surprisingly, Robert accepted Willie's offers of support without protest.

"Yea, I need to sit down, thanks Willie for looking out."
"Well, that what big brothers are for ... looking for the younguns."
Although Robert wanted to scream at his older brother for his belittling comment, he had other more pressing things on his mind—like the possibility of being a father. Without understanding why, he turned to Willie and asked, "With all of this talk about Dad, what type of father do you think he was?" "What kind of question is that? He was a great father."
"Who was a great father?" Jamie asked as Daniel.

Robert became quiet; he knew why he really asked Willie the question, but he did not want this discussion to get out of hand like the earlier one.

"Dad," said Willie, "I think Dad was a great father."

"Yea, because he worshiped you ... the great late baseball star."

"That could be true ... that he enjoyed the idea that I played baseball, and played it well ... very well, but ... I still think he was great ..."

"To put up with our mother, he had to be great."

Laughter broke out between the brothers, a rare moment when they had found a common foe.

Mrs. Turner finished her business with Mrs. Bray and bid her good-bye. She slowly stood up, *Finally got rid of Mrs. Bray, trimming the trees of the tree lawns my ass, she just want to talk about those awful ass children of hers, dammit. If I were her I would take all of their clothes, put them in a paper sack, set it on the porch and lock the freaking door. Sheesh ... My boys never gave me that much trouble.*

Mrs. Bray had stopped by for a little chat about the possibility of getting the city to trim the trees on the tree lawns. Because Mrs. Turner is the Street Club President, neighbors often stopped by to complain about something. Since the boys rarely require her assistance in their lives, Mrs. Turner had looked for other pursuits over which to wield her influence. One of those pursuits was obtaining the presidency of the 114th Street Club. In the Turner fashion of never exposing yourself foolishly, Mrs. Turner had made sure that she had enough votes to win before volunteering to run for the office.

To her surprise, no one ran against her and therefore she was awarded the office of President. Although she was the President of the Street Club, Mrs. Turner was far from being a happy woman. Her ability to influence others outside of the house was a poor substitute for her former position of power over the boys.

Mrs. Turner looked across the street thinking, *It's time ... them boys seems to be just milling around doing nothing* She stopped at the bottom of the steps to steady herself. Mrs. Turner knew that she did not move as quickly as when she was a young girl, but today she noticed that her movements were even slower.

Old age had not treated Mrs. Turner gracefully. Since her parents died when she was young, she missed out on their counsel about the three companions of old age: pain, time, and loneliness. Many days she had the will to defeat the loneliness monster, but the physical pain of living was something she was not prepared to face. No amount of pain pills or sore muscle ointment could successfully defeat pain's presence in Mrs. Turner's body. Pain met her early in the morning when she woke up and is her trusted companion throughout the day. Her companion has caused her to slow down and re-examine her daily routine. A discussion between mind and body had decided that chores such as dusting every day, like she did ten years ago, were a thing of the past, and dusting once week was a better goal. Old age and pain had stripped her of that enormous reservoir of energy that she was known for as a young child. No longer did Mrs. Turner have the desire or the ability to clean the house from dawn to dusk, naw … a little cleaning here, a little dusting there, and a nap in between had become the new way of life for her.

Although she appeared to take great pride in the inspection of the garden, what Mrs. Turner really liked was the attention that her boys gave her. As much as she disagreed with their choice in women, she had little influence over their decision-making. Her suggestions about what they should do with their lives appeared to fall on deaf ears. Her sons' responses to her inquiring questions were short and vague. She felt like she was being ex-communicated out of their lives, little by little. But the garden was the glue that brought her sons back again and again to her. As much as it seemed to the boys like their mother enjoyed nitpicking about the garden, she did not. She believed that the more she acted like a drill sergeant, the more of their collective attention she would receive, which made her feel good. Nothing could be done correctly in her eyes: there was always was a crooked row or a missed blade of grass that would send her into a frizzy and the boys back into the garden, grumbling under their breaths.

The brothers gathered at attention as their mother approached the garden with her head shaking back and forth. Mrs. Turner realized how tired she was feeling … not an aching feeling, but a feeling of being worn down.

As their mother made it across the street, the brothers positioned themselves at the gate: Jamie first in line, followed by Willie, Robert, and Daniel. Just as Mrs. Turner was about to open the garden gate, Jamie rushed to usher her inside the garden. He instinctively took her hand to support the transition from the sidewalk to the garden's bricked pathway. The brick pathway was completed right before Mr. Turner died. It was created from the bricks of the old apartment building that had been stacked against the fence. It was the last project that Mr. Turner and his sons completed together. Willie's watchful eyes observed something different about their mother's behavior that his brothers did not. He noticed their mother's steps were slower than usual, her breathing was heavy, and her body was swaying unevenly.

Willie nudged Rob and whispered in his ear, "Hey, Mama doesn't look well," but before Robert could reply, Daniel pushed his brothers out of his way, yelling, "Awww shoot, Mama—what's the matter? Maaaaaaaamaaaaaaa," as Mrs. Turner falls to the ground in his arms, and the birds began to sing.

CHAPTER 14

Daniel

Mama … yes, she was a hell of a woman. Within her lies the ability to tempt your taste buds with the most delicious pineapple layer cake ever made, while at the same time to alter a child's life with a few well-placed words. That child was me and the words that she uttered to chart a new direction in my life were, "Boy, you are a strange one." When those words were spoken to a young impressionable boy by his mother, a complex subconscious psychological effect occurred—he believed it and behaved accordingly. Yes, I am different: not different in a weird way, but in the way that I follow the road least traveled, especially by an African American male. No, she did not suggest that I eat sushi, backpack through Europe, or date outside of my race. Naw, my mom, along with other members of my family, even tried to disown me because of some of those actions. But it was she who sent me down that road searching for diverse experiences to enhance a new meaning of life. She uttered those words to me one spring day as I sat in the in the kitchen looking through a magazine while she was drinking a Pepsi Cola, her favorite drink. I asked her a question about something; I do not remember the subject matter—it could have been skiing, sun tanning, or square dancing.

She replied without looking in my direction, "I do not know boy, black people just do not do those types of things."

It was that answer, and her response to my next question, that caused me to embark on a different road of life experiences. First, I proceeded to ask the forbidden follow-up question: "Why not?" If a child questioned an adult in my day, it was generally due to a brain dysfunction, lack of sleep, or just a desire to meet your maker. At ten years old, I didn't have any of these symptoms—I was just curious. After my mom beat me like I stole something, cursed me out for the next two hours, and made me stay in the house due to my disrespectful behavior, I realized there must me something about that other life that she didn't want me to know about. Stupid me, I was determined to find out what it was.

Anything that was part of my black experience I continued to embrace, but I now looked beyond it. For instance, sports. Yes, I played baseball and football in the park with my friends, but I also stumbled into soccer, a game that looked like kickball. Having discovered soccer, I became a changed person. I delighted in my discovery of this new game, which led to me spending time in the neighborhood library reading everything I could about soccer. My library research revealed that one of the greatest soccer players in the world was a man named Pele, who happened to look like me. What confused me was that Pele was from Brazil, a country that I had never heard about, and he was considered black even though he was not from America. I was dumbfounded, so I asked my dad—my source for information about the world—about Pele, about Brazil, and about the sport of soccer. Not the best idea.

At that time in Cleveland, there were two daily newspapers: the Plain Dealer, delivered in the morning, and The Press, delivered in the evening. Reading the newspapers after he ate his meals was one of my father's many pleasures. So you can understand what type of mood he was in when I began asking him about soccer. He looked up from the newspaper with that "What the hetch you want, boy?" look. He told me that yes, he had heard about Pele, but had never seen him play. Brazil was in South America, and there are black people everywhere. With that proclamation, Dad gave me a look and resumed reading the newspaper. In short, that was his way of saying that my audience with him was over, so it was time to go play. I scurried away like a mouse that had stolen the cheese.

My interest in the sport led me to start playing soccer in the City League and at the college level, despite the frowns, stares, and questions of many of my peers. Their response to me playing soccer paled in comparison to the reaction I received when I began to date outside of my race. Now the frowns and stares were accompanied with behind-the-back-whispers, accusations, and denials. Not surprisingly, my male friends found themselves in a difficult situation. They believed if they openly supported my dating choices, it would cause all types of problems within their own relationships, so they candidly questioned my sanity out loud while reluctantly supporting me in what I called the "He is our boy but we like black women" type of way. I kind of understood the position that my dating choices placed them in, and therefore I purposefully did not hang around them and their women while in the company of any of my non-black girlfriends. Meanwhile, my crazy family went running for cover. After one of my brothers informed my parents of my dating preferences, they instituted their own "don't ask don't tell" policy, long before the current armed forces version became popular. After the Thanksgiving dinner incident, my mother quickly added a "do not bring them to the house" provision to the policy. I believed that certain brothers enjoyed the negative attention that I received from my parents, since now their choices of mates looked better in my parents' eyes.

My reason to entertain the forbidden fruit was not based on lust or curiosity, nor was it research into the social mating habits of the races. It had to do more with interacting with individuals with similar interests and who enjoyed my company. There were a number of activities that my group of friends had little desire to participate in. So in my attempt to meet my needs, I sought out individuals who enjoyed engaging in those activities. Good, bad, or ugly, these individuals were generally outside my racial group. Yes, I admit there must be some African American females who enjoy classical music, ballroom dancing, or bungee jumping, but unfortunately I did not know them.

My first interracial date occurred in church, the most segregated place in America. Well, maybe you would not call it a date, it was more of an interaction, but it was a special moment for me. You see, when I was a kid I attended the neighborhood church, The First Assembly of God, which I later found out was the white counterpart of the Pentecostal church in America. I was selected to be in the annual Easter Sunday school play as one of the two angels who stood before the tomb of Jesus. The other angel was Maria. To my seven-year-old eyes, she was the finest angel that God could have created. My heart burned for her. Being my shy and awkward self, I was unable to express to Maria my infatuation toward her, which in the end was probably better. During rehearsals we would speak and smile at each other, and once I touched her hand—wow, what a feeling. My moment of puppy love only lasted a brief time after the play ended. The neighborhood was becoming too black for most of the white church members; therefore, the church decided to sell the building and move to the suburbs, along with my precious Maria. Jungle fever did not rear its head again until after my college days.

After I graduated from college with my degree in education, I desired to widen my knowledge of the world with some type of international work experience. I wanted to join the Peace Corp, but I was scared. It had nothing to do with going to a strange, far-away place, nope—my fear had to do with telling my father that I was going somewhere in Africa for two years to help some poor people out. I could just imagine what my father would say to me after hearing my reasons for wanting to join the Peace Corps,

> "Boy, has you lost your mind? If you wanted to work with poor people, that fine, but your Africa can be right here in Cleveland."

My father was the type of man who was the happiest when he knew that his sons were employed. In his mind, being employed meant that an individual was earning his keep, but working for nothing was frowned upon. Therefore, the Peace Corp idea would not go over well with him. Determined to get my international experience and still receive the blessings of my parents, I decided to lie. Lying to parents is not healthy or encouraged behavior. I can remember when I was younger when one of my silly brothers would lie and get caught. You would have thought that all hell had been let loose. In my parents' eyes, there was nothing lower than a liar. So we learned at a very young age it was better to get in trouble by telling the truth rather than escaping judgment for a moment but getting caught in a lie later. On second thought, I truly do not believe that we stopped lying to our parents, but over the years we did it less frequently and became better liars. Although my brothers viewed me as the rebel of the family, the approval of my parents had always been important to me. I have always sought it, and at times their approval was quite slippery to obtain. I do not know what motivated me to deceive them, but I did. Well, I told them I wanted to go to Europe to study abroad for a year, but in reality, I wanted to hangout in Amsterdam to check out the happenings. Why Amsterdam? One of my well-traveled friends said it was the city of free sex and free drugs, and that was enough info for me.

A couple of strange things happened in my quest for an international experience: my parents gave their approval, I never made it to Amsterdam, and I fell in love. I believe their approval was an attempt to save me. After I graduated, America was still at war with itself and others. A transformed racial consciousness of America's black people had begun to manifest itself through a new set of behaviors and rhetoric causing white America to be on guard. It was an exciting, though dangerous time to be black. Change was coming, but at a cost. A young black man could easily become a statistic on a police blotter, especially one with a militant nature like me. In an effort to prevent one of their children from being a victim, they let me go. I knew their approval would come without any financial assistance, so in their minds, other than sacrificing their son to the European's hoards, it would not cost them a dime.

So using my money saved up from my summer job as a playground supervisor, I was off on my European adventure with the first stop being Paris, the City of Lights. I thought being in Paris would be an excellent test of my six years of French and an assessment of whether it had been a good investment. Well, I found out quickly that I got cheated, with no refund in sight. My French was stiff, clumsy, inaccurate, and embarrassing. The more I tried to speak, the worse I sounded, but thanks to the generosity of some English-speaking French people, I was able to obtain a hotel room and order some food. One eventful rainy day I visited the Musee d'Orsay, an art museum in Paris. My presence in the museum had more to do with getting out of the rain than to gaze upon the great masters. It is not that I dislike art—I just do not understand it, that is, if there is something to be understood. There I was, standing before a painting by Monet that looked like paint by numbers to me, when I heard a voice say, "Excuse me, are you okay?"

"Yea," I said slowly. "Why do you ask?"
"You have this strange look on your face, like you are sick."
"I just do not understand why this painting is considered art, and why it cost so much."
I finally turned my head in the direction of the voice and said, "Do you? And who are you?"

There stood Holly Wolff, an attractive French-Canadian with a distinct Jamaican accent who I later learned was studying art in Paris on a fellowship. She was wearing a white T-shirt with the saying, "Power to the People" on it and blue jeans. She held out her hand to shake mine, saying, "My name is Holly, and yes, I do. It's going to be all right—maybe we need to talk about art and the meaning behind some of Monet's works. There is a cafe down the street where we can talk and get some coffee, c'mon."

I don't know if I was more spellbound by her beauty or the gracious offer, but I followed this strange dark haired woman out the museum like we were old friends. As we walked down the avenue dodging raindrops, I asked about her T-shirt. Holly replied that she had picked it out because she liked the colors. I thought, *Who buys a T-shirt with those words on it for the colors? Yes, we do need to talk.*

During coffee in a nearby café, Holly told me that it was my distraught look of confusion that attracted her to me. My pained expression must have touched her heart, because from that moment until I left a year later she never shut up or was rarely absent from my side. I was soon to find out that Holly was the only child of an ethnically diverse union. Her father was a Jamaican-born postal worker, while her mother was French Canadian. Holly's parents never married. Due to the tension of having a racially mixed child out of wedlock, Holly's mother was forced by her parents to put Holly up for adoption. Holly's father interceded and took Holly to Jamaica to live with his mother until she was a school-ager. At six years old, Holly returned back to Montreal to live with her father, often going back to the island during school breaks. Holly stated that she does not know much about her mother, other than she died six months after giving birth to her. She learned over the years not to bring the subject of her mother or her "other family" up to her father. It was only until a couple of years ago that Holly stop wondering if every Montreal elderly white woman she saw was her grandmother. Despite her family issues, Holly excelled in school and had obtained a Bachelor of Arts and Masters in Fine Arts from McGill University while attending on full scholarship. She said that coming to Paris to study had always been her dream, and thus she was now living it. I was awed by her openness and willingness to take a chance. Those characteristics made her, in my eyes, a powerful person. When I told her my story she seemed amused that I had lied to my parents. She asked me where I was staying, and I told her I had a room at a hotel for the next three weeks then I would be off to Holland. Somewhere during the conversation Holly stated that she had just lost her roommate and asked if I would like to share an apartment for the remainder of my stay in Paris. This offer surprised me more than the first one. Being a Turner man, I was taught to be suspect of any folks bearing gifts. After a moment to recover, the opportunistic thought of saving some money reared its head and I heard myself saying,

"Are you sure? We just met."

"Well, I think I'm a good judge of people, and you need a place, and I need a roommate, and anyway if you try something funny, I know karate."

"Mmm … Okay, thank you for the offer. I need to see the place first, and we need to come up with some rules if I decide to room with you."

She smiled and said, "No problem; the flat is just around the block."

As we walked toward her flat familiar voices began to flood my mind. Yes, I hear voices and no, I am not crazy—I don't think. I have always heard them since I was a boy. They surface to encourage, discourage, and confuse me. This time, I heard my parents: *Boy, have you lost your mind? Open your eyes, she's got so much mixed blood in her she might be crazy, no good will come of this.* As usual, I disregarded what Freud would call my superego attempts to control my decision-making. But between the dissenting voices of my superego, another voice spoke to me, and it said, "*Trust her: you will do good-bye her.*"

The voice was from my childhood, one that I have learned to trust and obey. It was my crazy Aunt May talking to me, something that she did every now and then. Since her funeral, which I was unable to attend, I have felt her presence with me. I can remember sitting under the mulberry tree with her one summer night, upset that my pet frog had died. She leaned toward me, gave me a kiss on my head and said, "Daniel, those who you really love have the ability to become part of you. So do not be sad when a loved one dies, because they have the power to be with you in spirit always."

At eight years old, it is difficult to understand half of what is being said to you, especially about dead things. You need to remember that I am a sane person, college educated, minored in psychology even, but

I have learned to believe in spirits. Surprisingly, the first time I heard the voice, I knew it was Aunt May. It was like she really never left me, but just changed how we communicate with each other. Initially I was scared of the voice, and I thought that I was going crazy. But after twenty years, I have grown accustomed to hearing her raspy voice in my head when I am at the crossroads of making a decision. On that day, Aunt May's voice had penetrated my consciousness—which caused me to break out into a smile so silly that Holly asked me if I was all right. I assured her that I was fine, took her hand, squeezed it, and placed a kiss on her right cheek while I silently said, "Yes, ma'am," to my aunt's spirit.

Thus began a new chapter in my journey. My time with Holly was a journey into introspection. I learned a lot more about me than I thought was humanly possible. For the first time in my life I chose to tolerate someone in my space—which was really their space—for twenty-four/seven. My college roommate experience was one thing, but living with a female is a whole different world. There was also a dependent aspect of the relationship that was new to me. With my French being terrible, my knowledge of Europe nonexistent, and my financial status laughable, I found myself needing Holly more than I thought that she needed me. Little did I know she feel the same way about me. Much later she would tell me that she needed me more than I needed her. She saw me as a warrior with no fears, while she was afraid of everything. Holly was amazed how I did not allow the everyday stresses of life to overwhelm me. She needed me to be strong for her. The feeling of being dependent bothered me at first. Being in control was one of the major tenets of being a Turner man. Daddy's favorite saying was,

"Always be in control of your destiny."

Darn it, I was only fourteen years old when those very words were spoken to me. How did I know that those words were not to be taken literally? I guess that was the lesson that Dad wanted me to learn for myself. He knew if I internalized the words into behavior

I would face some difficult lessons about life. The result would be a series of humbling life experiences, one that I am encountering now. The dependence and the tolerance issues bored daily into my consciousness, causing feelings ranging from being blessed that I found such a wonderful woman to pitying myself for not being able to take care of myself. Unbeknownst to me, this began my reconstruction of my view of what it means to be a man.

I do not know when the friendship turned into a romantic relationship. I never said to Holly "I love you," but I knew in my young foolish heart that I did. What is love anyway but a strong positive feeling toward someone that causes you to exhibit perfectly illogical behavior because of how you feel toward them? Simply stated, I just liked the way she made me feel when I was around her. The more we were around each other, the better we felt, it seemed. I do not know if it was the lack of expectations or what, but for one year and a couple of days it worked—almost too well.

Although being with Holly was pure joy, we did have our moments of misunderstanding. How we communicated our needs to each other was quite different and at times proved to be very taxing. Holly generally expressed herself through indirect messages, which for an in-your-face person like myself could be quite confusing. As an example, one day Holly suggested that we spend a day at Claude Monet's garden in Giverny, a town outside of Paris. I must admit that I was looking forward to the trip. My connection to the earth has always been strong, and getting out of that crowded city to interact with Mother Nature was just what I needed. We took a bus to the garden that was full of American tourists, which allowed me to feel at home for a moment. They were friendly, chatty, and their mannerisms familiar. I wondered as they brought me up on the happening in the States if they would be this chatty with me if we were on a bus together in Cleveland. Probably not, but what does it matter—sometimes familiarity brings together strange bedfellows. I could remember the first day of my communication class of over two hundred students, and all five of the black students sat together, even though we did not know each other from Adam—the power of familiarity. We finally arrived at the garden, said our good-byes, and set out on our day communing with nature.

As we walked around these huge beautifully designed floral gardens alive with color, I smiled and thought, *This is art painted by my Creator.* Holly asked me what I was smiling about. While looking into her eyes, I said, "Being around all things that are beautiful—especially you."

She smiled and squeezed my hand. We had a quick lunch of sandwiches, sliced apples, and a glass of wine. Along with being a student of art, Holly is a word master, and every now and then she would asked me a crazy question about the meaning of a word. That day's word was romance.

> "So what is romance?" she said. "Romance?"
>
> "Yes, romance. What is it?"
>
> "Mmm … Good question." I felt her eyes on me as I struggled to compose an answer to her question.
>
> "Well, what is it?"
>
> "Romance. Well, I heard about it … a mystical something of the sort."
>
> She laughed. "Mystical something? Such a typical male response."
>
> "Well, does it exist? I mean, is romance reality based or something that Hollywood made up?"
>
> "It exists. It's a word. But it seems that you do not know what it means."

At this point I was frustrated and confused. Why the word romance? Is romance lacking in our relationship? Is she looking for romance or is she writing a poem about romance? *Shoot*, I thought, *I'm screwed.* In my anxiety-driven state, I attempted to save face,

> "You are right, I do not know what romance is. So please, tell me." "Silly, it is what we do for each other."
>
> "What?"

Spending a year in Europe taught me something that living all my life in America did not have the ability to show me. My eye-opening discovery: race might not matter. Not surprisingly, history and my life experiences had taught me the opposite. You can have a wonderful childhood, attend the best schools, have an outstanding job, but race matters in America. So being forced to come to grips with American's reality at a young age, I chose to take advantage of my blackness. I strategized how to use my race. As a badge of honor, a reflection of a force of nature, something for the majority culture to deal with and not to forget. My transformation occurred during my college days, when I posed as a pseudo-black nationalist. Since I grew up in a black neighborhood, being black lacked uniqueness and therefore possessed little in the way of power in the hood. But being black at a large, white university—it was easy to be someone that you were not. I took pride in using my minority status as a way to shake up some people's racial consciousness and to expose their hidden guilt. If there was a situation or a discussion on campus where being black made my white peers uncomfortable, I was there. I wanted them to acknowledge my blackness, understand their white privilege, and to never make me feel invisible again. "Power to the People," I would say, and they were mine. Then I traveled to Europe and lost all my perceived powers to come into a new understanding of how the world turns.

I can remember when it occurred; it was one day very soon after I had arrived in Paris. I was walking down the street next to my hotel when I saw two dark-skinned individuals who had the physical characteristics of African American men back home. In other words, they looked black. So as we passed each other I nodded at them … and nothing, no response.

The nod, the simple up and down movement of the head, a nonverbal way of addressing another African American male has the power of making an individual feel alive. The brief nonverbal gesture by another male indicates that you are a person worthy of recognition in society that attempts to make you invisible. You need to understand that in America the "nod' that the black males give to each other is unspoken recognition. In African American culture, you do not need to know the other male, but if you nod at them, you get a nod back. This nonverbal bonding ritual of head nodding is specific to the African American male culture and is not seen in the majority culture. After the first set of "brothers" did not respond to my gesture, I thought nothing of it. So I tried the nod on a lone brother who was approaching, I nodded—and again, nothing, no reciprocal greeting or acknowledgment. My research continued throughout the day with negative results. I received no return nods, just strange looks from my black brothers. I felt isolated, unable to bond spiritually and connect with another black soul around me. Not surprisingly, the white Europeans just ignored me; they did not even look in my direction. There was no fear in their eyes, no conflict of the soul. They just made me invisible. Alas, a frightening truth began to emerge. My power, the power that my racist American majority gave me was void outside of the US of A. I came to find out that it was in Europe that one does not derive power over other by the color of their skin—it was through language. Since my French was poor, my true power was nonexistent.

My time in Paris with Holly can be summed up in a Phoebe Snow tune called "No Regrets."

> No regrets although our love affair has gone astray No regrets I know I'll always care thou you are away Somehow our happy romance ended suddenly
> Still in my heart you'll be forever mine
> No regret because someone looks good to you,
> No regrets sweetheart no matter what you say or do I know our love will linger when the other one forgets
> Still in my heart you'll be forever mine.

The summer was coming to an end and the day finally approaching. Holly's fellowship was over, the lease on the flat was up, and it was time for me to go home. We knew the day was before us but little was said because, well possibly, we did not know what to say. When I met Holly good fortune suddenly remembered me, and my life became much easier. I found a job teaching French students English—not a bad job, as it was an English Immersion program where only English could be spoken in the classroom, which was right down my alley. My education degree was finally paying dividends. Good-byes have never been my strength, darn it, I use to cry when I went away to college. I was not looking forward to saying good-bye to Holly. Our situation was simple, yet quite complex. We began with a chance meeting with no expectations other than mutual respect, but within a year's time, we had acquired so much more.

Friday was the last day of classes for summer session. Unknown to Holly, I had purchased a ticket to go home on the following Wednesday. The upcoming weekend would be my last with Holly in Paris, and I was planned a special dinner to celebrate and to discuss the future. The day started off as usual: we had coffee and toast for breakfast and rode our bikes to the university. Before going our separate ways, I reminded Holly that we could not meet today as usual for lunch because of a scheduled staff lunch. After our "have a good day" kiss, Holly stated in a soft voice that she loved me and walked away. Surprisingly, at that moment I did not think much about what she said because that is how I was feeling. But something caused me to replay that moment during lunch, and I realized that she had never said that she loved me before. I could not wait to get back to the flat to ask her "why" about this morning's moment. With a bottle of red wine, a loaf of bread, summer sausage, an assortment of cheeses, and cake, I left work early to prepare the feast. But the feast turned out to be dinner for one because Holly was gone, leaving only a card in her place. She wrote:

Dear Daniel

Thank you for being a wonderful roommate, friend, and lover. I have learned so much about myself by being with you. I'm sorry that you reading this card instead of me talking to you. But I am not as brave as you, and since writing this hurts so much, I know that facing you with those big brown eyes of yours would have been an impossible task. As I look back over our time, I knew that I loved you from the day we met. It was our time. Labeling what I felt about you scared me so I did what scared people do. I have left … but after experiencing the most wonderful man in the world.

Love, Holly

That was it …

I did not know how to feel, whether I should be mad or what. So I sat in the kitchen, uncorked the bottle of wine, poured a toast to the experience of love, and cried until I was awoken by birds singing in the morning.

CHAPTER 15

The Birds

Mrs. Turner awakens to a sound like birds singing. *Yes, those darn birds have woken me again,* she thinks. The sound that Mrs. Turner initially thinks are birds she soon comes to realize is instead a choir of many voices, singing in the far off distance. As she listens quietly, the singing becomes louder and clearer. She smiles—the song is a familiar one. The choir is singing a song that she sang many times as a child. It is one of those songs that if you allow it, it has the ability to transform your present situation into one that allows peace to stand still. She begins to mouth the words softly while instinctively swaying to the beat. The song reconnects with something deep inside of her, and she becomes one with the music. With her hands lifted toward the sky, the power of the voices raises Mrs. Turner up and she takes her place in the choir of many voices, singing,

Swing low sweet chariot Coming for to carry me home Swing low sweet chariot Coming for to carry me home I looked over the Jordan

And what did I see

Coming for to carry me home

A band of angels

Coming after me

Coming for to carry me home ...

The song resounds softy within Mrs. Turner, and she feels utterly at peace. *What beautiful voices,* she thinks. Gradually, an image of her past appears before her. It is the very image that has haunted her since she left the south. Surprisingly, this time it does not scare her, nor does she run to hide. She meets the monster face to face—the monster she has unknowingly created herself from a mixture of fear, hurt, and pride. Mrs. Turner looks into its eyes ... she does not see a terrible creature, but a scared child with big brown eyes whose journey had been scarred with human suffering. She sees herself. As tears flow down her face, the choir then begins to softly sing,

Precious Lord take my hand Lead me on

Let me stand

I'm tired, I am weak, I am worn

Through the storm, through the night, lead me on to the light

Take my hand Precious Lord Lead me home ...

The boys watch as their mother lies before them on the ground in the garden, under the shade of the mulberry tree. 911 has been called, the sound of the sirens fill the air as the ambulance approaches. A gentle breeze travels through the garden, accompanying the singing of the birds. Time takes on another meaning. The neighbors gather outside the gate, pointing, questioning, and giving their spin of what is going on. While the brothers stand in shocked silence, a smile appears on their mother's face before life decides to leave her body ...

Soon, I will be done with the trouble of the Lord going home to live with God ... sang the Choir

Hope, then the absence of hope. They remember that their father told them that the "absence of hope" results in death. Collectively, the brothers' spirits inform them that their mother is passing over. The ambulance arrives, and a great rush of humanity moves toward the garden. The paramedics shout questions at them, but the brothers do not respond. They hold each other's hands as tears run down their faces. Instinctively, they close ranks with arms around each other. As the paramedics attempt to resuscitate their mother, the brothers give their spirits permission to tell their story of loss thru vocalizations of pain, while the wind blows, and the birds sing.